The Spotlight.

Roxy Jacenko is the powerhouse behind Sydney's hottest fashion, beauty and lifestyle PR firm, Sweaty Betty PR. Not only do the products she publicises make the pages of every magazine in town, but so does Roxy herself. It's rare to see her away from the social pages. She starred in 2013's *Celebrity Apprentice*, and her profile is only going up! Read Roxy's bestselling Jazzy Lou novels *Strictly Confidential* and *The Rumour Mill*.

The Spotlight.

A JAZZY LOU NOVEL

ROXY JACENKO

ALLEN&UNWIN

SYDNEY • MELBOURNE • AUCKLAND • LONDON

First published in 2014

Allen & Unwin
83 Alexander Street
Crows Nest NSW 2065
Australia
Phone: (61 2) 8425 0100
Email: info@allenandunwin.com
Web: www.allenandunwin.com

Cataloguing-in-Publication details are available
from the National Library of Australia
www.trove.nla.gov.au

ISBN 978 1 76011 144 1

Typeset in 12.5/18.5 Joanna MT Std by Bookhouse, Sydney
Printed and bound in Australia by Griffin Press

10 9 8 7 6 5 4 3 2 1

for my mummy x

1

I'm guessing it was the first – and probably the last – time a bomb squad has been called out to detonate a sex toy. In my defence, it was my husband and his overly active imagination who thought the buzzing noise coming from the box left on our doorstep sounded like an explosive. Okay, the Eastern Suburbs of Sydney aren't exactly a prime target for terrorists, but at the time I had recently made an enemy of a Russian businessman with possible links to the mafia, so it wasn't that illogical a leap. Mysterious box – must be a bomb. Let's be honest, if it was going to happen to anyone, it would happen to me. That's why when my husband Michael shook the box then yelled, 'Ruuuuun,' I ran like a supermodel for a cupcake after a Fashion Week closing party.

In hindsight, I must have looked hilarious. Just imagine, Australia's premier fashion publicist, Jasmine Lewis – the owner of luxury PR consultancy Queen Bee – sprinting down the road like a James Bond extra. Oh, except I was dragging a toddler and a Birkin handbag. I also like to think I have better dress sense than a Bond girl. Who wears a black leisure jumpsuit? Pleeease. How try-hard! For me, it's all about hi-lo dressing – if you want to wear leather then tone it down with a sports tee.

Note to self – I'd have to let Miu Miu know their high-top trainers are not only super cute but also bombscare-proof. I outran Michael even though I was wearing four-inch wedges. They should start supplying these bad boys to the Australian armed forces.

When Michael called the police, I was surprised they took it so seriously. As my husband hollered down the phone, 'We're under attack!', I wonder whether the emergency-services operator did a quick record search of our names. Are eighteen parking fines in six months enough to put a girl on the most-wanted list?

Luckily, my daughter Fifi thought it was all a game, while the three of us huddled behind a neighbour's Mercedes, me expecting to see smoke billowing from our driveway at any second. As the police cars got closer, Fifi sang along with the sirens: 'Nee naw, nee naw. Join in, Mummy!' I really needed to start limiting her TV time and maybe delete the 'police chase' channel from our Sky Box. For an almost two-year-old, she seemed far too comfortable with drama, and totally at ease with the mayhem unfolding around her.

In my opinion, it was a little excessive sending six squad cars and a police helicopter, which circled our house so low that it blew the cover off the swimming pool. Perhaps it was a slow crime day, or they just don't get many bomb scares in suburban Sydney, but it seemed like every cop in the city turned up on our doorstep.

'They'll probably do a controlled explosion,' Michael assured me as we peered over the car's bonnet, watching a bomb disposal expert creeping down our driveway behind a transparent shield. Apparently my husband was now an explosives expert as well as an investment banker. I didn't point out that his entire knowledge of bomb disposal was gleaned from episodes of 24. Anyway, what did I know?

'Umm, yeah. They'll just cut the red wire, right, with a pair of those nail scissors . . . or something,' I replied. I didn't have a clue, but I'm a firm believer in faking it until you make it.

When it comes to knowledge, my specialist subjects are somewhat superficial. I can recite the names of every designer to have shown at New York Fashion Week, spot a knock-off handbag at a hundred paces, and know how to blag my way into any marquee in the Melbourne Cup Birdcage (not that I need to, as I'd hope I'm on the VIP guest list). I also have an inbuilt homing device for high-end shopping spots. Drop me in any city in the world and I'll hunt out a Louis Vuitton store, without any wi-fi reception. However, none of these unique skills would be helpful in our current situation, so for once I remained silent. I watched and I waited as the team of experts entered my home and, after twenty tense minutes, exited in a huddle with one of them carrying the box as gingerly as a newborn baby.

As we huddled behind the car in our combat position I saw a guy approaching who resembled the lead actor from *Entourage*. You know, the one with the eyes you could swim in. What was his name again? Adam? Adrian? I was itching to Wikipedia it, but this was neither the time nor the place to pull out my iPhone.

I guessed that Adam/Adrian was head of the bomb squad, because he was wearing a black bomber jacket with a badge on the chest that read 'Explosive Ordnance Disposal'. I'd actually seen a very similar jacket on the Ksubi catwalk at last season's Fashion Week. In an odd way this brought me some comfort. If we were about to die, at least I'd leave the world in well-dressed company.

I suddenly had a thought – what was the last thing I'd posted on social media? I know how newspapers work and how lazy journalists are when it comes to research. With any dramatic death, whether it's a murder or a car crash, they simply drag your last words from Twitter and your last photo from Instagram. Front page done! That's why, before I step foot on a plane, I always make sure I tweet something reflective and intelligent ('I am officially over the phrase "so blessed". It appears that it's taken over from "I know, right?". Eugh. LOL'). I also make sure I Instagram a flattering picture. It could be the last memory of me if I cark it.

I needn't have worried, as it didn't seem like the bomb squaddie was bringing bad news. In fact, Adam/Adrian seemed to be on the verge of laughing, unless that twitch of his lip was caused by anxiety. 'You three better come with me,' he said, offering me a hand, which I refused. I may have been crouched in the gutter, but I have my dignity.

As we obediently followed our saviour towards the house, I noticed that all the other police cars were leaving. See ya then! Clearly we were no longer a priority, which was surely a good sign – or else they were giving the bomb a wide berth.

We were ushered into the back of an unmarked white van. On the floor of the van was the bright yellow shoebox we'd found on our doorstep, wrapped in the remains of a black ribbon. I hadn't really got a good look at it before Michael sounded the alarm. It didn't look very 'bomby'.

Another of my special skills is being able to recognise the gift-wrap of every major department store in the southern and northern hemispheres, just by its colour scheme. I can pick out Tiffany blue, Fortnum & Mason green and Bloomingdale's brown in an instant.

That's why I instantly knew this box had come from Selfridges, which is my favourite department store in London. This is mainly because I'm obsessed with the candy section in the food hall. Where else can you buy a pair of Jimmy Choos, elderflower marshmallows and vodka lollipops under one roof? Either these bombers had good taste or we may have jumped to the wrong conclusion. I had a growing suspicion it was the latter.

'What the hell is that?' asked Michael, peering into the box, which he'd approached cautiously.

Adrian looked at me with one eyebrow raised. 'The boys and I think we've identified it,' he replied. 'But maybe your wife can give us a second opinion.'

Why was he asking me? I struggle to program the DVD player, let alone decipher a weapon of mass destruction. But, hey, maybe I'd uncover hidden talents. I did once untangle twelve hundred gold charm necklaces which had arrived from the manufacturer in a knot harder to unpuzzle than a Rubik's Cube.

So I approached the box, pushing up the sleeves of my cashmere jumper. I half expected to see a grenade, or at least a mass of red and blue wires. But . . . this wasn't what bombs looked like in the movies. For one, it was presented so nicely. Nestled in the box, on a bed of baby-pink tissue paper, was a gold metal gadget shaped like an oversized jellybean. As I peered more closely, I noticed two words engraved in the side: 'Lust Personified'. Was that a . . . ? No, it couldn't be . . .

The van had fallen silent as the men waited for my expert analysis. I cleared my throat and, glancing at Fifi, lowered my voice as I answered. 'I can't be sure, officer, as it's not exactly my area of expertise, but I think that's a vibrator. Yes, yes, I'm pretty sure it is.'

As I learned later, when I checked on the Selfridges website, this wasn't just any vibrator. It was by Lelo – the most expensive makers of 'intimate lifestyle products' in the world. The model I had in front of me was worth $5500, but the most expensive vibrator they sell is made of twenty-four-carat gold and has a price tag of $15,000. That is one pricey orgasm.

'Jazz, did you order this?' hissed Michael. Bloody cheek! I may often forget to eat lunch and frequently freeze my iPhone by putting in the wrong pin code but I never, ever lose track of my internet shopping. And I certainly wouldn't forget ordering a $5500 vibrator.

So who had sent it? If this were a gift from a brand it would have been sent to the Queen Bee offices. Then I noticed an envelope sticking out from beneath the tissue paper. How had the bomb squad missed the gift card? Seriously!

I ripped open the envelope and read the card aloud:

Jazzy Lou, I saw this and thought of you. If you want a job done well, do it yourself. Love and kisses, Shelley

I should have guessed! Only my oldest and dearest friend Shelley Shapiro would be cheeky enough – and also wealthy enough – to splash out a few thousand dollars on a novelty sex toy. Raised by a single mother, who died when Shelley was eighteen, my BFF and partner-in-crime had been left with a bottomless trust fund – and a fiercely independent streak. She lived by the motto: 'You don't need a man when you can buy happiness.' Her main occupation, as noted on visa documentation, was 'shopper', although she'd recently started adding 'fashion conservator' to confuse customs officials.

Shelley was my most trusted confidante and the only person who knew that my marriage was going through a rough patch. Despite the fact that we'd only just passed our one-year anniversary, the honeymoon period was a distant memory. This was not something I wanted to make public knowledge.

I put a lot of effort into maintaining a perfect public front. When Michael joined me at VIP functions – which he did less and less frequently – I had mastered our red carpet 'loving couple' pose (my hand on his shoulder, our feet pointed towards each other).

I know I shouldn't care what other people think, but this is Sydney, the home of keeping up appearances. Also, I was sure that Michael's ex-girlfriend Belle Single analysed every pap photograph of us, looking for signs of wear and tear. The pin-up had too much time on her hands since her reality TV show had been canned. If you were one of the few people to watch it, you might have noticed she still has a photo of Michael stuck to her fridge. Really, girl, get a grip!

This is why I would never admit to anyone besides my best friend that my relationship had all the pizzazz of an X Factor reject. Our sex life in particular was less than explosive (excuse the pun), which explained the motivation behind Shelley's surprise present. Later, my best friend insisted it was sent as a joke after a few too many martinis. This was classic Shelley! In the same intoxicated online shopping spree, she'd also ordered a $6000 Dior watch and a Harry Potter wand from Harrods' kids' department. She gave me the former as an apology, and Fifi got the latter, which became her favourite accessory.

Unfortunately, the bomb scare had ongoing consequences – especially to Michael's ego. Apparently, your wife's sex toy becoming the talk of the Australian police force is emasculating. Come on, bud! This is the twenty-first century. Cameron Diaz has told the world about her vibrator. For fuck's sake, Jennifer Lawrence admitted that a maid once found a box of butt plugs under her bed. Even if I had bought it myself, every woman is allowed to experiment.

But my husband is more prudish than the average celebrity. Michael saw the gift as a slight to his manhood. And, naturally, the news made the next weekend's newspapers, thanks to gossip columnist Wally Grimes, who always salivated over my mishaps. (Note to self: I still have to find out which of my neighbours leaked the story and get my revenge, possibly by posting negative feedback on their eBay. Hah!)

Thank goodness that bitter twisted old queen Wally only got half the story, and didn't find out exactly what was inside the parcel. Still, he made the most of his sparse information: *WHAT A BOMBSHELL! Socialite-cum-publicist Jasmine Lewis sparks bomb scare with her shopping haul.* If there's one thing I hate it's being called a fucking socialite. I am an entrepreneur, thank you very much. I run a multimillion-dollar business. Don't lump me in with the Paris Hiltons of the world.

That little incident also meant that Michael and I were placed on the emergency services' blacklist of time wasters. *FFS, Shelley!* Just imagine it — Australia's premier fashion publicist listed alongside a woman who once called the police because the power cut out in her apartment and she was worried her Sara Lee gateau would melt (true story). That is not the type of exclusive club I want to be a part of . . .

There was one positive repercussion of the bomb scare – I now had an excuse to redecorate our house. Well, I really had no other option. Despite the fact that the mystery package was left on our doorstep, the bomb squad had crashed through the house in both directions. The cream carpet was covered in muddy footprints, there was a dent in the patio doorframe and, as I tried to explain to Michael, it just felt . . . traumatised. And I wasn't the only person who thought so.

'Eeesh, you poor baby,' soothed my new interior designer when he came to inspect the damage. But he wasn't talking to me, he was talking to the bricks and mortar. Jackson Saunders is the absolute best in the interiors business and had spent the past three months in Los Angeles, designing Perez Hilton's playroom. Because of his celeb-heavy CV (and the $5000 Armani suits he wore even when painting), I could overlook the fact that the flamboyant creative had a . . . new-agey way of working.

The moment I'd opened the front door to Jackson and invited him in, he'd put his ear to the wallpaper in the hallway and listened intently. Oh god, was that a tear rolling down his cheek? 'Jazzy Lou, this house is troubled,' he shrilled. 'We're just going to have to change it all. There really is no other option!'

Jackson calls himself an 'interior delighter' and believes every house has a soul and must 'give birth' to its own colour scheme. The owner just has to cough up the moolah.

I usually have little patience for this kind of mumbo jumbo, but Jackson's portfolio was stunning, despite his unusual way of working. He was currently on his hands and knees on the hallway carpet, his eyes closed. 'I can feel your house's heart beating,' he mewed. 'My darling, your house needs interior therapy – stat!'

'Are you thinking a few tweaks here and there?' I asked, already knowing the answer was not going to be in the affirmative. Jackson was famous for his extreme makeovers, which were the interiors equivalent of Demi Moore's pre-*Charlie's Angels* cosmetic surgery. My house would be unrecognisable when he'd finished.

I glanced over my shoulder to the living room where Michael was listening to a podcast on his laptop. Thankfully, his noise-cancelling headphones meant he hadn't overheard us. My husband had recently developed an obsession with an American motivational speaker called Chad Turner (you might have seen his TED talk on 'extreme board meetings'; he once flew his entire workforce to Everest Base Camp for a brainstorm). I think Michael had a corporate crush, although I wouldn't say it to him. At bedtime, his nose was always stuck in a copy of Chad's business memoir, and I noticed he'd started speaking in Americanisms. The other day, I'd actually heard him bark down the phone, 'The difference between "try" and "triumph" is just a little umph!'

When it came to redecorating our $6 million home, I'm guessing that Michael would argue I had a little too much umph for my own good! You see, Jackson wasn't the first interior designer I'd hired since the bomb scare. Almost a year had passed, and during that time the entire house had already been overhauled by two separate interior designers – one after the other.

Okay, refurbishing an entire house twice in twelve months might sound excessive, but this was my sanctuary and I needed it to have the right feel. I'd made a mistake the first time around by placing my hopes – and my credit card – in the hands of a young designer called Jessica Salmon. You might remember her from the last series of *The Block*, where she turned a derelict semi into a property that sold for $4.5 million. In comparison to that I thought our palatial home would be a doddle, but it hadn't lived up to expectations.

It's not that she did a bad job exactly, it's just that she seemed to forget my house wasn't the set of a television show. Yes, we do require that dividing wall, Jessica. I appreciate that it's breaking up your 'vision', but it's also holding up my ceiling. And no, I'm not prepared to sleep in a hammock because a bed doesn't fit in with your safari theme.

I'm all for aesthetic value, but it also has to be practical. Since when does a $2000 lamp not require a power socket? According to Jessica, the lamp with its plaited silk cord neatly coiled under the table didn't need electricity. It was just a feature to be oohed and ahhed over. Presumably while I flicked through the pages of one of the coffee table books she positioned on the coffee table. Apparently I was meant to spend my evenings reading Valentino's memoir in the dark.

That lamp was the final straw. When my lah-di-dah deco-rator had suggested the lights were just as fabulous without power, I decided to quit while I was ahead and start over. Was Jessica offended when she found out I'd two-timed her with Jackson? I have no doubt. But she handled it graciously enough, thanks in part to my overgenerous tip, and moved out her ladders to let her competitor's in.

To be honest, I wish she'd trashed the joint in a jealous rage, as it would have been easier to explain to Michael why I needed a do-over.

It's not that Michael could quibble about the expense. The cost – now escalating rapidly – was coming out of my pocket and not his. As a wife, I do not believe in joint bank accounts (or joint Facebook accounts, just for the record). I was the one bearing the brunt of the outgoings, although I was trying to keep costs to a minimum as much as possible. I was pulling in favours left, right and centre for discounts on couches, wallpaper and the huge antique brass bathtub that Jackson insisted we have in the corner of our bedroom (yes, bedroom).

We were also taking Michael's needs into consideration and had ordered a custom-made 'watch safe' for his collection of Rolexes, which had a glass window at the front so you could see the watches spinning on miniature pedestals. I was slightly worried it wasn't the safest safe, but Jackson insisted it was art, and any thief would respect that and therefore not steal it.

So, if it wasn't the cost, what was getting Michael's back up? Well, it was more the inconvenience of sharing our home with a pack of builders (sorry, Jackson, I mean 'house whisperers'). The first time around, under Jessica's reign, my husband had taken to sleeping at the office because he said the paint fumes gave him a headache.

He was only away one or two nights a week but it was another sign of chinks in our relationship. How different it was from the early days of our romance. When I'd first 'acquired' my husband from Belle we hated spending any unnecessary time away from each other. Now the incompatibility of our busy work schedules was sometimes a blessing, as it gave us less time to argue.

Married life. What can I say? Every day is a challenge and it's certainly not all a bed of roses. When you throw together two intelligent individuals with high-powered careers who deal in profits that look like telephone numbers, there is never a dull moment. Chuck in a toddler too, and you might as well set off a container of firecrackers in your living room.

Perhaps I should have been more worried about the declining state of my marriage, but I had too many other distractions. My life was spinning around faster than a better-known Minogue sister. As well as the double house redecoration, I was putting plans in place to revamp Queen Bee PR, moving it firmly into the twenty-first century.

A lot of businesswomen would be frazzled, but the truth is I'm comfortable with change – maybe a little too comfortable. This may sound harsh, but I don't believe that anything is forever – even relationships. I'd just hoped that when I got married, I would be proven wrong.

2

'Lulu!' I yelled at my long-suffering assistant. 'Why do I have seventeen crates of guava-flavoured vodka in my office?' Out of interest I opened a bottle, took a swig and then spat it across my desk. It tasted like cheap kiddies' lip gloss. FFS! That aftertaste was going to stick.

'Oh my god, Jazz, I'm so sorry.' Lulu sprinted into my office, her blonde hair pooling around her shoulders. 'I meant to have these moved by the time you got in. The couriers left them here by mistake. They're from the Dutch Courage distillery in the Hunter Valley – an experiment gone wrong, apparently. They have litres of the stuff and want to know if we can think of a publicity stunt to shift it.'

I groaned. It was only nine o'clock on a Monday morning and already I was in damage-control mode. 'Okay, this is what you do,' I barked. 'Call that mixologist from the Star casino. The one who accidentally melted my Miu Miu clutch with his flaming martini. He owes me a favour. Tell him to start spruiking guava vodka cocktails to any celebrity who goes in there. I need to make this shit trendy.'

Lulu, rapidly typing notes into her iPad, let out a whistle. 'But Jazzy Lou, it tastes like expired Halloween candy,' she protested.

'Well, he'll just have to get imaginative.' I picked up a bottle and peered at the ingredients, then grimaced. 'I don't care if the cocktail is one percent guava vodka and ninety-nine percent orange juice. We just need to be able to say the coolest party people are drinking it: Delta, Jen, Joel Madden . . . We tip off the fashion mags that there's a new It-drink in town and boom, it's an overnight sensation!'

As Lulu scurried off to guilt-trip the mixologist (that's what you get for igniting my precious Miu Miu), I wondered how my career had come to this – flogging sickly-sweet liquor.

When I started Queen Bee PR ten years ago, I had vowed never to represent a product that I didn't genuinely love, or at least like. I wanted our headquarters to be an extension of my character. If I wouldn't wear it, eat it, drive or drink it, then it didn't have a place on my client list. I have integrity, dontcha know! Plus, as everybody in the PR world understands, it's a doddle to make the world excited about something when you're genuinely enthusiastic about it yourself.

Since then, thanks to a lot of hard work, Queen Bee PR had grown into an unstoppable monster. It's something I would never have thought was achievable as the student who had excelled in ticking every 'absent' column, was constantly described as 'disruptive', and scored fourteen percent in maths for her school certificate, before getting turfed out of school in year ten. I was proud of my unexpected success.

Yet recently, a number of less-than-tasteful brands had been slipping through the net and onto our client list. The guava vodka was a good example. Why had I lowered my standards? One word – money! That thing that used to grow on trees in the fashion world was now disappearing faster than a Tasmanian rainforest.

I blame the credit crunch, or an epidemic of stinginess, but some of the larger, global brands had slashed their publicity budgets to practically zero. Last week, a bigwig from the makeup brand L'Atitia had had the cheek to ask if she could pay for our services with free lipstick. Seriously! They made a profit of $8.3 billion last year, and they wanted to pay me in makeup. If I hear the phrase 'contra deal' one more time I'll scream. Let's not beat around the bush – you just want me to work for nada.

The interesting thing was that while the big boys were slashing their budgets, the small fry seemed to be doing the opposite and were on a publicity drive. Okay, they weren't all high-end products, but at least somebody still realised that a PR rep was a worthwhile investment. When a distillery that produces alcohol which tastes like kerosene is willing to pay you $20,000 a month to promote their products, it's very hard to turn them away.

Luckily, the magazine editors, who I needed to plug these products, were also lowering their standards. In the past, I would never have dreamed of sending Lillian Richard, the snotty editor of *Eve Pascal* magazine, anything but the finest Brut champagne. Now, though, she'd be getting a bottle of guava vodka – and she'd probably be thankful for it.

Just as L'Atitia's publicity budget had dried up, so had the endless freebies editors were once showered with. In the old days, an editor would screw up her nose at any gift that wouldn't earn her more than $300 on eBay (those who say they don't flog their freebies are lying – or missing an opportunity to make a fortune). In the old, opulent days, any editor would have at least two interns (referred to as fashion cupboard monkeys) who were employed just to unpack the gifts sent by fashion labels and designers. You've seen *The Devil Wears Prada* – it really isn't much of an exaggeration. Now that times were tougher, fashion designers were happy to loan out samples but actually asked editors to send back the outfits afterwards – and even pay for them to be dry-cleaned.

And it wasn't just brands tightening the purse strings; publishers were too. At a recent party, I'd overheard Rochelle Crawford, the editor of *Bizarre* magazine, complaining that she'd been called into an emergency meeting with their finance department. 'They're monitoring my company credit card,' she whined. 'I'm only allowed to spend $200 on taxis per week.' The *Bizarre* offices were split between two buildings at opposite ends of the same street, and it was a well-known fact that Rochelle hailed a taxi rather than walking the 500 metres between them. 'They even said I should share a taxi with my staff if we're going to the same event,' she added. 'Can you imagine? I don't even like sharing an elevator with them!'

The day after I overheard Rochelle's rant, I received an email from the lifestyle editor of *Bizarre* just 'letting me know' they'd decided to add a monthly car review to the magazine. They'd just LOVE to include my client Porsche, who were apparently Rochelle's favourite car maker. In fact, Rochelle would LOVE a long-term loan of the latest model . . . and could we cover petrol too?

I feel like Santa freaking Claus sometimes, fulfilling the wish lists of journalists struggling to live upper-class lifestyles on working-class salaries. Oh, how I'd love to tell the fashion diva to stick it, but I'm a professional and I couldn't pass up the publicity opportunity. I did fantasise for a moment about emailing her a link to Gumtree's second-hand car section, with some 'affordable' transport options. Let her arrive at Fashion Week in a clapped-out rust bucket that leaks petrol over her Manolos.

I'm not usually this vindictive (well, not often), but Rochelle would deserve it. This is the woman who once said to me, in front of the head of Gucci, 'Everyone knows that PR is just the fallback plan for failed journalists. Right, Jasmine? If you can't break into the world of fashion magazines, PR is your plan B. Every fashion publicist really wants my job.'

I pride myself on my discretion, and so I bit my tongue. But it wasn't easy, as I had a comeback locked and loaded. Little did Rochelle know that I'd been approached by her boss six months before to see if I was interested in editing a new weekly fashion magazine. I'd politely declined – even before he apologetically revealed the salary. To paraphrase Linda Evangelista, I wouldn't get out of bed for that amount. Who was Rochelle kidding? My assistant Lulu was on practically the same wage, and my second-in-command Anya was on double that salary.

I've been accused in the past of being a cut-throat boss with zero compassion (well, that's how one ex-employee described me in a recent lawsuit). Yet Anya, my longest-serving Bee, is proof that if you keep your nose to the grindstone, working for me does pay off. Anya has just bought a $1 million house in Double Bay, where she stores her convertible Mercedes in the undercover car park. Her wardrobe is even bigger and brassier than mine (remember I also have a toddler with expensive taste in clothes).

The Queen Bee headquarters, in the thriving suburb of Alexandria, is a twenty-minute drive from the centre of Sydney. Don't be fooled by the warehouses that surround our building. Anyone who is anyone knows that Alexandria's industrial estate is home to the hottest photography studios in the city, where every fashion magazine descends to shoot their editorials. Our leafy street is a thoroughfare for supermodels on their way to pose for *Vogue* (or whichever mag has booked out the studios that day). We're in prime position, in the suburb where the magic happens and dreams are made.

I like to imagine that our palatial office is what heaven will look like if God is a fashion fan. Within the clean white open-plan warehouse is rack upon rack of the latest ranges from the hottest fashion labels, ready to be loaned out for fashion shoots or to socialites who need a killer outfit for an event.

Out of my thirty or so staff members, the majority are female, but it's not because I'm sexist. Fashion PR is generally a female-heavy industry and it's no coincidence that my office sometimes looks like a clone factory, with thirty blonde heads bent over their HPs. My staff arrive at Queen Bee PR as fat girls and go out as thin girls, with expensive cars and apartments in the most exclusive areas of Sydney.

If I ever post a job vacancy on social media, we're over-whelmed with applications from girls who follow my life on Instagram and think PR is all parties and schmoozing celebrities. They want to be me (poor cows!), but many of them only see the glitz and glamour. I work twelve-hour days, six days a week, and even when I'm technically off duty I'm still permanently 'on'. I have 'iPhone elbow' from checking my emails while lying in bed, and have even asked Jackson to install a speakerphone in my shower as part of the makeover, so that I can multitask washing with conference calls (just for the record, it will not have video function).

Speaking of telephones, I always carry two mobiles with me, and as Lulu left my office, one of them started ringing. All of my Bees have at least two mobiles. In any other industry this would seem somewhat suspicious, but we genuinely need to double-up our devices – one mobile for VIP clients, one for general business calls, friends and family.

The phone currently trilling from my handbag was the latter, and the screen flashed with a photo of Shelley, blowing a kiss at the camera.

'Jazzy, what are you wearing?' This was my best friend's standard greeting, like a caller to a late-night adult chatline. But the only salacious details Shelley was interested in were the names of the designers I was wearing.

I looked down at my outfit and rattled it off from head to toe. 'Balmain, Givenchy, H&M and Chanel ballet pumps. The cream ones.'

I heard Shelley's earrings rattle down the phone as she nodded. Now that I'd received her fashion approval we could start our conversation. This is how our relationship goes.

'Babes, you are utter perfection,' she enthused. 'So, what's new with you? You sound kind of down. Is everything okay?'

This is why Shelley is my best friend. I'd spoken less than ten words but she knew me well enough to sense I wasn't my usual perky self.

I sighed. 'Just a bad morning at the office. I don't mean to complain, but I sometimes feel like I'm losing my mind . . . not to mention my dignity.'

Case in point, I was currently wearing a product made by one of my clients. It was a new bra from a shape-wear brand, which claimed to make your boobs go up three sizes – instantly. I'd ordered all the Bees to wear them, so that we could become walking billboards for our product. PR can sometimes feel like prostitution without the sex (celibacy seemed to be an ongoing theme in my life right now). You spend every day begging, borrowing and stealing just to get some column inches at any cost.

I recounted the guava vodka debacle to Shelley, who after a decade as my confidante has a working knowledge of PR by proxy. 'Today has already been a freaking nightmare,' I moaned. 'How far can you massage the truth before you forget what you really believe in?'

Don't get me wrong, I still love working as a publicist, but being your own boss is not as alluring as it sounds. If Coca-Cola asked me to head their publicity department I'd jump at the opportunity. It would feel like a holiday representing one corporation, rather than juggling the ridiculous expectations of a hundred brands and countless B-grade celebs desperately seeking freebies.

Shelley tutted sympathetically. 'Babes, you're just having a wobble. Is your blood sugar low? Why don't you send Lulu out for some cronuts? Do you need a fashion pick-me-up? I just got a delivery from Net-A-Porter and those Chloé linen shorts I ordered have come up so small. They must be a faulty batch. Come over after work and grab them.'

This was Shelley's solution to any problem – high-calorie food and high-end fashion. The first unfortunately stopped her fitting into the second. My best friend has reverse body dysmorphia and is convinced that she's a size six, even though she's closer to a size fourteen. This is why most of her purchases find their way into my wardrobe, as she's far too wealthy to know the meaning of the word 'refund' – and she's also far too generous to send her purchases back when she can gift them to me.

Sadly, neither fatty food nor fashion could solve my current career issues. 'I'd love to but I can't tonight, Shells. I have to work on my new business plan,' I replied apologetically. 'If my new venture is going to be ready to go next month, I've got some serious hard graft ahead of me.'

A girls' night was long overdue, and an evening spent raiding Shelley's cast-offs was always appealing, but I had a new baby to attend to – and I don't mean Fifi.

Can you keep a secret? I had decided to overhaul my business, and move away from fashion and lifestyle brands and into celebrity management. It was an area I had been considering for a while but I'd put the idea on the backburner. I've always been put off the idea of working with D-listers such as Belle Single and Sydney's other homegrown 'talent' like occasional model (and constant bogan) Samantha Priest. Australia's celebrity scene isn't exactly Oscars-worthy. As soon as a local actress or singer gets onto the first rung of stardom, they hop onto a plane to Los Angeles to schlep with Hugh Jackman and Chris Hemsworth. So much for loyalty!

So why was I suddenly prepared to move into people management? Because there was a new breed of celebrity taking over the scene – bloggers! A blog is no longer seen as the thing you do if you can't get a 'real job' writing. The underdogs of the internet had risen to greatness and had the potential to earn themselves a fortune.

I'd been watching the steady ascent of bloggers for the past year or so, waiting to see if their status would continue to rise. This was a multimillion-dollar business if you knew how to work the system. In this town and across the world, bloggers are the new celebrities, much to the annoyance of the 'old' celebrities, who can't understand why they don't have the same currency.

The Sartorialist, Scott Schuman, sells advertising space to American Apparel and Net-A-Porter for 'a good fraction of a million dollars'. How incred is that? And when Topshop opened their latest store in Sydney, they weren't clamouring to clothe the cast of *Home and Away* (sorry, guys). They were sending out free swag to online mavericks such as Sydney Fashion Blogger and the duo from Doncha Wanna Be Us. I had already reached out to both bloggers and organised a coffee meet-up to discuss signing them up.

My friend Shay works for the biggest advertising agency in Sydney and summed up the sea change perfectly: 'No brand wants to be aligned with a celebrity on a pedestal. They want someone their customers can relate to. It's cool to be normal.'

Of course, when these brands say 'normal' they don't really mean it. They don't actually want their billboard girl to be an 'average' Australian (size sixteen, bad roots, shops at Supré). It's just like when a fashion brand wants to hire a plus-size model. Real women? Not likely. All too often, rather than hiring a size-sixteen they hire a size-twelve girl and then make her wear a fat suit. A little padding on the hips, a lot of padding on the boobs. They don't really want 'real' – they want a fembot with Victoria Beckham's legs and waist, but Scarlett Johansson's curves.

This is why fashion bloggers are so appealing. They straddle the gap between 'normal' people and celebrities. Oh, you think you can dress like them, but just try copying the outfit of a blogger like Nicole Warne from Gary Pepper Girl. You can buy all the components, but you'll end up looking like a dog's dinner. That's okay – you can just live vicariously through her daily blog posts. And the more fans a blogger gets, the more they can charge for advertising. We're not talking small change either. Fashion blog The Refinery made $25 million last year. Show me the money!

It would be a brave new world for Queen Bee PR. My plan was to still represent a select few of my fashion and lifestyle brands but do a mass cull of the rest. I intended to pour the majority of my resources into The Talent Hive, which is what I'd decided to call Queen Bee's new division. Cute, huh?

My reincarnation wasn't public knowledge yet. I'd only told Shelley, Michael and Anya, because I couldn't risk the news being leaked. But I planned to say a polite goodbye to forty of our current clients. However, deciding who to keep and who to cull was proving more difficult than I'd first thought.

'It feels so weird purposefully trying to get rid of clients, when we put so much effort into getting them in the first place,' confessed Anya during one of our late-night planning sessions, as we showered Byron Bay Cookie crumbs over our keyboards. At least when I ditched some of our food brands, we'd have fewer snacks in the office to tempt us.

I knew what Anya meant. I did feel odd – though pretty smug – choosing whom to wave goodbye to after so many years chasing clients. Now the shoe was on the other foot, as I was sure many of my clients would be devastated when I gave them the boot. (Speaking of boots, I was keeping the Balenciaga account!)

For the past three weeks, Anya and I had stayed behind in the office when the other Bees left for the day. A normal clocking-off time for my staff could be 9 pm, so Anya and I were practically sleeping under my desk. I felt like a teenager trying to choose her favourite schoolgirl crush as we wrote lists of pros and cons for the clients we were deciding between.

Cocobella Coconut Water. Pro – Miranda Kerr loves it. Con – how many ways can you respin a coconut water story? Juicy Joo watches. Pro – the editors at the fashion mags loved the bright colours. Con – everyone who wore one got a nasty rash from the cheap plastic.

'Add both of these to the reject list,' I told Anya, who made a note on her laptop., 'Can you pull up my diary? I need to arrange a face-to-face meeting with every brand we're giving the shove.' I wanted to tell them the news personally. I wasn't going to wimp out with a Dear John email.

'Your schedule is pretty packed over the next couple of weeks,' replied Anya. 'You don't need time for eating and sleeping, do you?'

She was only half joking. It was 10 pm and next to my keyboard was an untouched slice of toast with vegemite which I had planned to eat for breakfast. My schedule was even busier than usual, because as well as my usual duties, I had meetings arranged with numerous bloggers I wanted to sign up. I was eyeing off some veteran bloggers who still had life left in them, and the rising stars I could sign up early (and cheaply) just before their profiles took off.

I wasn't going to focus solely on fashion bloggers either – there were also the beauty bloggers, travel bloggers and health bloggers like Fitilicious (that body, those abs!). And let's not forget the fashion 'moggers' (that's male bloggers) like Front Row Suit and D'Marge, both of whom I had a major sartorial crush on. I also planned to sign up Jackson as my first interiors blogger. The Talent Hive would be a one-stop shop for brands who wanted to collaborate with an online megaphone. There's no publicity like a blogger with 100,000+ followers on Instagram.

'Jazzy, do you think you have enough . . . experience to focus on bloggers?' asked Anya, who has been with Queen Bee PR since day one so has earned the right to be candid.

I could understand her concern, as I'm not exactly technologically savvy. I have been known to refer to social media as 'The Facebook' during meetings with clients, and suspect that Fifi knows her way around my iPhone apps better than I do – although that may be because I sometimes use it as a replacement babysitter when I'm held up in a meeting (only as a last resort!).

'My love, I don't pretend to know it all,' I told Anya. 'But don't sweat, sweetie. When I started Queen Bee, I didn't have a clue about running a business. The secret is surrounding yourself with people who do know the answers.' That's why I planned to bring in Gen Y-ers who actually know what HTML stands for.

I may not understand the workings of a computer but I am the master of faking it till you make it. During my career, I'd gone from selling burgers in a McDonald's drive-through (I supersized more orders than any other employee) to selling million-dollar diamond rings to the wealthiest women in Sydney and then owning my own business. No way was I going to let something as minor as a lack of know-how stop me from jumping on the blogging bandwagon – and I planned to be in the driving seat. There was no time to waste, either, as this trend wouldn't last forever.

Here's one thing you should know about me – I am obsessed with being the first to do everything, as I know from experience that you have to get in early and get out just as quickly. The bloggers I planned to sign certainly had a shelf life, and I intended to chew them up and spit them out before they turned sour.

3

'That's it. I cannot live like this anymore,' I wailed. The last
straw was when I leaned against a doorframe and got a stripe
of 'eggshell' paint down the back of my new Josh Goot dress.
I looked like a skunk . . . albeit a very fashionable one.

And so I made a decision – the two of us were going to
evacuate until the refurbishment of Casa De Lewis was over.
When I say 'the two of us', I'm talking about myself and
Fifi. When I'd cornered Michael in the kitchen one morning
to tell him about our relocation, I thought he'd be relieved to
escape the mayhem too, but I was mistaken.

'I actually think I'll stay here,' he replied, pulling a bottle
of Nudie juice from the fridge.

Fifi is the only person in our household with a supply
of solid food in the fridge. Since we moved into our house

the week after we got married, neither Michael nor I had prepared a single meal in our fabulous kitchen. What? We're busy people. Plus, have you seen the prices at Whole Foods? It's just as cheap to eat out or get takeaway.

'I don't like the idea of a bunch of strangers having free rein in our house,' added Michael after taking a gulp. 'I think I should be here to keep an eye on them.'

At that moment a builder walked past outside the kitchen window, narrowly missing smashing the glass with the wooden plank he was carrying. I had to admit Michael had a point. I swear I caught one builder eyeing off my Birkin collection as he measured up my walk-in wardrobe. Luckily, when it comes to bags, I only do oversized. Just try smuggling one of those bad boys out in your toolbox.

Yet I was still slightly offended that Michael was happy for me to move out without him, even if our separation was only temporary. It's not like we were ever together in our house during daylight hours; these days, one of us was always asleep by the time the other got back from the office.

'Fine, whatever,' I said. 'If you need me you know where to find me.' He'd clearly made up his mind and I wasn't going to try to convince him.

My husband raised an eyebrow. 'Oh, come on, Jasmine. Don't carry on. You're the one who's doing a runner. *And* you're the one who brought Armageddon on our house in the first place. I didn't even think it needed to be changed – I was happy with the way it was to begin with.'

Of course you were, I wanted to shout. *You're Mr Groundhog Day!* This is the man who, once a year, bulk-buys twenty Tom Ford suits. He has also signed up to a subscription shirt service, which means that at the start of each month he is mailed thirty identical Dolce & Gabbana shirts. He has no issue with repetition (and, you could say, no imagination). His focus is on convenience. We are very different animals, but they do say opposites attract, right?

Despite Michael digging in his heels, I was excited about our temporary relocation to a hotel. It might sound excessive, but it was cheaper than hiring another house for three months. And the only other alternative was staying put, sleeping in a hard hat and steel-capped boots. Not freaking likely!

My favourite book when I was growing up was *Eloise*. Do you remember it? It was about a six-year-old girl who lives in the 'room on the tippy top floor' of the Plaza Hotel in New York, with her pug dog and a turtle. During my last trip to New York, I'd taken Fifi on a guided tour of the suite they've dedicated to the fictional character. She was so taken by it (okay, I was so taken by it) that Jackson was going to remodel Fifi's bedroom at home based on this suite. It would have an Eloise-inspired palette of pink, black and gold leaf and feature a signature Plaza chandelier, with crystals shaped like candy canes. It was my own childhood fantasy, made possible thanks to my adult workaholism. Candy-cane crystals don't come cheap!

If we lived in the Big Apple, I'd have happily shelled out to stay at the Plaza for the estimated three to six months it would take to complete our reno. Luckily, Sydney has no shortage of luxury accommodation either, and I'd chosen the Four Seasons Hotel, overlooking the harbour with views of the Sydney Opera House. Yes, I would be joining the esteemed ranks of the 'long-termers' (that's how hotel managers describe the guests who stay for a while, sometimes sticking around long enough to have suites named after them). My monochrome idol, Coco Chanel, lived in The Ritz in Paris for more than thirty years and even died in her suite, which she'd had redecorated with her own furnishings. Hopefully Jackson wouldn't take that long to complete his interior masterpiece.

'What an appropriate moving-day outfit you're wearing, Jazzy Lou,' said Michael with more than a touch of sarcasm as he watched Lulu and me struggling to load eight giant suitcases into the back of my Jeep. A courier from the hotel would also be arriving soon to collect a pile of storage boxes containing my accessories.

I didn't know why my husband was mocking my outfit. This Givenchy dress was sports luxe and so totally practical. Okay, I'd teamed it with strappy Valentino stilettos, but I was a pro when it came to heavy lifting in high heels. It's all in a fashion publicist's job description (along with an ability to sip champagne for hours on end at press events without getting drunk).

Anyone who thinks you don't do manual labour when you're the head of your own company is very much mistaken.

Okay, some bigwigs refuse to get their hands dirty but I'm not one of them. As a boss, I'd never ask my Bees to do any task I'm not prepared to do myself.

Just yesterday, I had to schlep up all 1504 steps of the Sydney Tower carrying twenty-four gift bags because the elevator had malfunctioned. One of my newest clients – a local Cross Fit school – held a special class on the top deck. Imagine the health editors of every women's magazine trussed in safety harnesses, trying to heave barbells above their heads. It was certainly memorable. The Queen Bee gift bags are legendary, and these ones weighed a ton, as they included a Lululemon yoga mat, a pair of Nike high-tops and a real coconut. I didn't actually need to take part in the Cross Fit class, as bringing the bags up those stairs was workout enough.

It's all in a day's work. I'm frequently found on my hands and knees unpacking boxes in the Queen Bee showroom (to the amazement of my accountant, who was confronted with the sight of my butt when he last came to visit). That's why I love my Alice Temperley biker pants with the leather patches on the knees, as they give me more padding when I'm acting as a dogsbody.

'Umm, you could always help, you know,' I huffed at Michael as I heaved the cases into the car. 'We're schvieting over here.' My husband was leaning on the bonnet of his silver Mercedes, scrolling through his iPad, wearing aviator sunglasses and a bored expression. He hadn't offered to lend a hand even though we were obviously struggling.

Poor Lulu was particularly red in the face, although that was mostly because she was wearing a thick Bottega Veneta sweater in thirty-two-degree heat. I had offered her a cooler tee but my assistant, a dedicated follower of fashion, and refused to get changed despite the blazing sunshine. 'It's limited edition and dip-dyed,' Lulu argued. 'I'm never taking this beauty off, like, ever!'

Sometimes I'm not sure if I'm a good or bad influence on my protégées. I once fainted at Sydney Fashion Week when the air-conditioning broke during Ellery's show and I refused to take off my Saint Laurent leather jacket. I'd been on a six-month waiting list for this baby and wasn't going to waste a moment to show it off. Even when I was lying flat on my back on the floor that jacket looked great. I figure I pioneered 'unconscious chic'.

'How can size-zero clothes weigh so much?' groaned Lulu as she crammed a hatbox into the boot of my car beside a plastic crate marked 'flats', which was significantly smaller than the crate marked 'heels' (there were also boxes marked 'midi', 'sandals' and 'sneakers').

If I'm honest I may have overpacked a little. My Goyard luggage pile made Rachel Zoe look low maintenance. However, I maintain that my haul only contained the essentials I needed for my day-to-day life: Chanel ballet flats in six colours, my collection of vintage *Vogues* for inspiration, and my travelling spray-tan booth – I haven't seen my natural skin colour since about 1999. And in my defence, five out of the eight suitcases belonged to my toddler. Despite being less than a metre tall, this mini fashionista in the making did not pack lightly.

Now that Fifi was nearing her second birthday, she was starting to show a personality as strong as her mother's. While most toddlers have tantrums over what they want to eat or which dolly to take on a car ride, my daughter's terrible twos revolved around her fashion sense. She had very firm ideas about what she would and wouldn't be seen out in – and they changed faster than Belle Single's boyfriends.

On a good day, I found Fifi's reluctance to wear any dress with spots or any shoes with a buckle (her current fashion no-nos) amusing. On a bad day, I was seriously concerned I was raising a diva to rival Jennifer Lopez. If she grazed her knee, even her bandaids had to be colour-coordinated with her clutch bag (yes, my daughter carried a clutch, containing a Juicy Tube lip gloss and one of my old credit cards).

It was all my fault, really. It's not like Fifi had stocked her walk-in closet out of her own pocket. I was clearly her enabler. I'm just thankful that Net-A-Porter is yet to launch their children's website Petit-A-Porter because I think I'd be bankrupt by now. There are just *sooo* many treasures to buy for little girls. I have to admit that in the first eighteen months of Fifi's life I may have gone a little OTT when it came to filling her wardrobe. If you'd looked at her bedroom, you'd have thought I'd given birth to triplets, as every corner was crammed with Gucci onesies and Dior sleeping bags.

When I look back at some of the 'must-have' items I bought my baby daughter they seem ridiculous. I mean, what newborn baby can wear suede driving shoes? And matching driving gloves? I laugh when I look at some of the most expensive items I bought, as they were totally impractical. One puke or wee through a nappy and they were ruined. (And dry-clean-only baby clothes? Really?) I bought her a $2000 cashmere onesie that I now view as a work of art, rather than an item of clothing.

So I can't blame Fifi for having expensive tastes. I'd created the two-year-old fashion lover. Anyway, I was happy in a way that I was raising a child with high standards and strong opinions. Although I had recently cut back on my junior-designer shopping habit and was trying not to overindulge as much on Fifi's wardrobe. I'm not made of money – although I am good at making it – and needed to rein in my spending to balance our long-term hotel stay.

I shouldn't have let Fifi be present in the room when I packed her (five) suitcases, because she was soon micromanaging me. Even though she's only just beginning to put together sentences, my little girl has a knack of getting her own way without even speaking. She has her mother's 'poison-dart' look down to a tee, and shoots it at anything or anyone she disapproves of. Including me.

As I packed Fifi's ensembles into her suitcases, she picked over my selection, crying, 'No, Mummy, no. Silly Mummy.' I put an outfit in, and she pulled it out again, throwing dresses, pants and socks into a reject pile. She then toddled around pulling alternative outfits from the shelves of her walk-in wardrobe. Imagine Carrie's dream closet from *Sex in the City*, if it was hit by a shrink ray.

Fifi's wardrobe is arranged in alphabetical order by designer (Burberry, Dior, Fendi, and so on). I swear it's helping Fifi learn her alphabet, as I test her by naming a designer and asking her to point out that section. And that's not all – within each alphabetised category her outfits are also divided into season: no sleeves, short sleeve, long sleeve, et cetera.

According to Michael I have OCD, but I think I'm setting a good example for Fifi. These days, too many people look down on perfectionism like it's a bad trait. What's the problem in wanting things to be faultless? I happily admit that I'm very, very obsessive. I mean very. But I think that's what makes me a good businesswoman, and probably a good mother as well.

Finally, all the bags were crammed into the back of my Jeep, with the overflow filling every spare space in Lulu's leopard-print Alfa Romeo. The car had been wrapped for a publicity stunt which Queen Bee had organised and my young assistant had taken a liking to it.

When it was time to leave, Lulu discreetly waited in her tiger-mobile to give Michael and me some privacy to say goodbye. As I kissed Michael at the front door, I noticed he kept his eyes on his iPad screen, where he was reading an article called 'The rise of personal robots'. This was obviously far more important than farewelling his wife.

To my annoyance, I felt a flash of neediness. Why wasn't he more upset that his significant other was leaving? Even though I was only upping sticks to the other side of the city, and he had promised to come for sleepovers, shouldn't he at least feel . . . something?

'See you then,' I tried to sound breezy, while wishing that he'd put down the damn iPad. Was I going to become another statistic, one of those women whose marriage is broken up by technology?

My husband gave me a pat on the bum, which felt more like a shove than an affectionate gesture. 'Cool, cool, I'll drop by over the weekend,' he said distractedly. 'We can go out for dinner. Can you send an invitation request to my iPhone calendar to remind me? If it's not in my diary I might double-book you.'

Umm, was he kidding me? He expected me to send a calendar request for our date night? This was the modern-day equivalent of a 1930s housewife having to call her husband's secretary to see him. I really didn't want to leave on a sour note, but I couldn't let this comment slide.

'Well, who said romance is dead,' I retorted, with an edge to my voice. 'In case you haven't realised, I am not one of your freaking clients, I am your wife. If you can't remember me without an alarm popping up on your phone, then we're in serious trouble.'

Michael looked at me doubtfully. 'Oh, don't exaggerate, Jazzy Lou,' he groaned. 'You're the one with the uber-busy life. I just meant that you should tell me when you're free and I'll work around you . . . Isn't that how our life normally plays out?'

I had a sense that there was more to this argument than a dinner reservation, but I also didn't have the energy to push the issue at that moment. I glanced at my Rolex. I was already running late and didn't have a free window in my schedule for a battle. So I plastered on my best smile and faked contrition.

'I'm sorry, Michael. I'm just agro with the move,' I soothed. 'Let's meet up over the weekend like you suggested. Cocktails in the hotel's bar? I've heard they do a mean martini and red cocktail and their Wagyu beef is to die for.' How depressing that I felt I needed to bribe my husband to meet me, with his favourite alcohol and hand-massaged meat.

As Lulu and I drove out of the driveway in convoy (I'd arranged for the nanny to drop Fifi at the hotel later, after I'd had time to settle in), I watched my husband in the rear-view mirror. Polishing the bumper of his Mercedes with his sunglasses cleaner, he didn't even look up as I beeped a goodbye and put my foot down on the pedal. The luggage in my car suddenly felt twice as heavy with the extra weight of my emotional baggage.

I was grateful when I pulled into the Four Seasons' car park and a team of porters appeared like magic to help me unload my life from the boot. Unlike my husband, they didn't look at all perturbed by the number of my suitcases. I heard one porter mutter to another, 'Long-termer,' and they looked impressed rather than judgemental.

As I went to pick up the smallest of my bags, a porter ushered me away. 'No, no, madam. We'll take that to your room for you.' I don't actually enjoy being fussed over too much, but I was paying a premium for the privilege so I figured I might as well make the most of it.

Even Lulu looked slightly taken aback, as – for the first time ever in my presence – she had nothing to do. 'Lulu, my love, you can clock off for the day,' I told her. She looked stunned, as it was 'only' 6 pm. In our line of work a nine-hour day feels like slacking off.

I followed the ants' trail of porters as they hauled my luggage to my suite, and deposited it neatly in the walk-in wardrobe after I insisted that, yes, I could unpack for myself. I must check the etiquette on long-term tip-giving. Surely if I stayed here for three months I wouldn't be expected to continue to tip every time my bed sheets were turned down or my fruit bowl was replenished? I'd have to ask Shelley – she always seems to know these things.

As the porters bowed graciously and exited into the corridor, I sat on the edge of my king-sized bed and breathed in deeply. The room smelled of Lumira candles – Persian Rose scent – which were burning in every corner. Either this was a coincidence or a hotel staff member had done their research and seen me post on my Instagram that these were my favourite candles. Now that was customer service! Let

Michael stay in a house full of paint fumes; I work too hard to live in discomfort.

As the door closed behind the final porter and I was left alone with my thoughts, I did feel guilty about our lovers' tiff. I am no stranger to confrontation, but that doesn't mean I enjoy it. I'm also not one to bury my head in the sand; instead I take an active approach to solving problems (that's why Queen Bee PR is so successful).

I retrieved my iPhone from my handbag, opened up my to-do list and under the 'urgent tasks' column added a reminder: *Rescue relationship*. Just typing it made me feel better, as at least I had good intentions, even if it was written on a to-do list with forty-seven other 'urgent' items.

I'd get around to it eventually. Probably. Hopefully. Michael wasn't going anywhere. Oh, how naive I was . . .

4

I admire any woman who has an entire hanging rail in her walk-in wardrobe dedicated to shorts, especially when they're grouped by fabric – denim, leather, silk, crochet. That's why the moment I saw the closet of Ebony Frith – one half of the fashion blogging duo Doncha Wanna Be Us – I just knew they had to be the first clients I signed up to The Talent Hive. Not to mention the fact that they get 700,000 hits on their fashion blog a month and have 480,000 Instagram fans. These girls weren't just pretty faces; they were business savvy and sitting on a potential gold mine.

If I'm honest, despite being an avid fan of their blog and having an almighty crush on their wardrobes, I fully expected to hate the girls when I met them in the flesh. My first impression of Ebony was from an interview I read in *Bizarre* magazine where she spoke about how she'd first discovered fashion when her mum bought her a Gucci saddle for her pony. She was five years old. Was I jealous? Maybe. Did I instantly google Gucci saddles and buy one for Fifi despite the fact she doesn't even have a pony? (It was now a very stylish clotheshorse in her bedroom, draped with her scarves and sweaters.)

Ebony and her blogging partner Tara Rain had been best friends since they met at boarding school in London (both sets of parents shared the opinion that an Australian education wasn't 'polished' enough for them). At the end of their $40,000-a-year education, they'd graduated with top marks in art and an intimate knowledge of the best vintage stalls at Notting Hill market (the rumour goes that Ebony pioneered the boho chic trend when Sienna Miller spotted her wearing a denim cut-offs and cowboy boot combo while standing in line for her espresso at Coffee Planet and asked to take her photograph).

Anyway, London hadn't managed to capture the girls' attention long term. They both craved the sunshine (we also share a tanning addiction); plus, when you have legs the length of Tara's it's a travesty not to live in a country where you can wear cut-off shorts all year round. So they'd both returned to their hometown of Bondi and nabbed jobs as visual merchandisers at competing fashion stores. Despite being professional rivals, their bond had never broken. In fact, every morning they'd email each other photographs of their outfits (subject line: 'Fash of the day'). What began as a bit of fun was now an online mood board with a cultish following, which they continually updated with their amazing ensembles.

I had big plans for DWBU and could easily think of a dozen fashion labels who would love to collaborate with them. I could already imagine an exclusive range of Doncha Wanna Be Us jeans designed with Paige. And possibly a range of smoothies with Tara's face printed on the label. Fact of life, it's far easier to market a person when that person looks like Elle Macpherson's younger, hotter sister.

I invited the duo to the Queen Bee offices and sent Lulu out for macadamia-milk lattes, which I knew from Facebook was their go-to drinks order.

'Girls!' I squealed as they walked through reception. 'Don't you both look gorgeous. Oh my gawd, I look like shit. I haven't washed my hair in a week. Look at me!' The hair comment was sadly true. My hair stylist had the flu and had cancelled my weekly wash-and-blow appointment. Do it myself – are you kidding me? I'm a dedicated blow-ho and learned a long time ago that a weekly visit to the salon is worth the investment.

I was exaggerating when I said I looked like turd, however. I've also learned over the years that the fastest way to a fashionista's heart is self-deprecation. Everyone is insecure in this business, no matter how confident they appear on the outside. Bigging them up and putting yourself down is an instant leveller, and my favourite ice-breaker.

'What are you talking about, Jasmine?' protested Tara. 'You're a hottie! Actually, can I take a photo of you for our blog? Will your assistant take it? We can all be in the picture together.'

Yes, I wanted to scream, *home run!* This was exactly the reaction I'd been hoping for when I'd carefully selected my outfit that morning (well, I *was* meeting blogging royalty). I'd gone for denim shorts, in Ebony's honour, along with a black tee from The Row, Balmain 'shoots' (shoe boots), and my favourite rose-gold Rolex watch, which always set off any outfit. And it seemed my selection had passed the litmus test. A blogger asking to take a photograph is the ultimate compliment.

I usually don't agree to spontaneous fashion shoots unless I know I'll get photo approval. Even if it's just going on social media, I want to be able to choose my best angle, crop out my problem areas, and select the most flattering filter. But I trusted that the DWBU girls wouldn't allow on their blog any photograph that wasn't aesthetically pleasing. And so I struck the pose I've learned makes my legs look slimmest (one foot crossed in front of the other, toes slightly pointed in). Within ten minutes of the picture appearing on their Instagram feed, along with my name and the hashtag #newfriendsexciting-plansahead, I had over 2000 new followers. It was further proof that DWBU had harnessed people power.

And to my surprise, I found I LOVED the girls. Sure, they lived in a fashion bubble, but don't we all. They couldn't help being born gorgeous, rich and stylish (humph!). And they seemed to be genuinely amazed and incredibly grateful that they got to do this for a living.

'Let's not pretend it's rocket science, Jazz,' laughed Tara once we were shut in my office with the door closed so the other

Bees couldn't overhear us. 'All we do is post pretty pictures. I wouldn't exactly call us entrepreneurs.'

'We just want to create,' added Ebony. 'All this talk of profits gets in the way of my process. I don't want to spend my time playing hard ball and making deals when I could be having fun styling.'

The best thing about bohemian creative types is they really don't like talking about money, as they prefer to think of themselves as 'artists'. This meant that even though the DWBU girls had the business savvy to manage themselves, they really didn't want to.

So they signed on the dotted line (in purple sparkly gel pen), and the three of us celebrated that night with lychee caprioskas at the Four Seasons bar, getting far drunker than I'd planned to. In fact, they both ended up sleeping in my hotel suite, and I heard Tara throwing up the next morning, which made me like her even more.

'Jaysus, I feel rough,' she croaked as she exited the bathroom. 'I'm never drinking again . . . Shall we order bacon sarnies . . . and Bloody Marys?'

There's nothing like shared hangovers to bond strangers together. We'd now become friends as well as business acquaintances.

It was time to press 'go' on The Talent Hive. A week after signing the girls, I made my business plans public knowledge. I gave the exclusive story to my old friend Luke Jefferson, who'd recently been promoted to entertainment editor at *The Sun* after many years writing their celeb gossip column. I'd known Luke when he was a twenty-two-year-old junior reporter writing lowly stories on school fetes for a local paper. Over the course of our careers we'd scratched each other's backs (and drowned our sorrows together) on many occasions, so I couldn't have been prouder of his recent promotion, even though it meant I saw him less because he was a man-in-demand. I still knew every detail of his life and of his frequent trips to Hollywood, thanks to his Instagram feed, which was a montage of selfies of Luke with the stream of bigwig celebrities he interviewed. And despite his new media stature, he was still interested in snippets of gossip from the Sydney scene and never, ever misquoted me.

'I'd LOVE to share your news with the masses,' Luke crowed when I called him. 'Can I mention you're living in the Four Seasons? They might give you a dissie for the publicity!'

I guessed he was on his way to LA (again) because I could hear a flight attendant in the background telling him to please turn off his phone as the plane was about to depart.

'That'd be great, sweetie.' I tried not to feel jealous of his jet-setting lifestyle. I could really do with a holiday. 'Shall I email you some quotes? If you run a photo, can you make it flattering, please!'

Luke laughed. 'Always, always, my beauty. Look, I've got to fly – literally – but can I tweet you next week? Hashtag air kiss.' This is how Luke speaks, like the ultimate Gen-Y stereotype, but he tones down the millennial slang when he writes. And he was true to his word, giving me a half-page spread in the weekend's newspaper and on *The Sun*'s website.

OUT WITH THE OLD, IN WITH THE NEW AGE!
Australian publicity powerhouse Jasmine Lewis has revealed plans to ditch half of the clients from her firm Queen Bee PR to focus on launching a creative agency called The Talent Hive.

According to Lewis, the forty clients she plans to drop will be replaced by bloggers and social media personalities. 'I am certainly not quitting the publicity business,' insists Lewis. 'I'm just bringing it into the 21st century.'

As soon as the story broke, every phone in Queen Bee headquarters started ringing off the hook, with calls from our current clients who were paranoid that they might get the boot (we were holding our cards close to our chest for now) and also from the waifs and strays of the Sydney celebrity scene who needed representation. Even though I'd made it clear in the press release that we were a creative agency, focusing on bloggers, photographers, stylists and makeup artists, that didn't stop every wannabe actress and singer from applying to be on our books. They didn't realise I had my wish list of clients written, and if you weren't already on my radar you clearly weren't worth chasing. Don't call me, I'll call you!

The girls from Doncha Wanna Be Us were proving to be a joy, especially Tara, who had become a regular visitor to the office. I suspected that she was lonely. Her right-hand woman Ebony had recently started dating an electrician called Jasper, who lived in a bedsit in Redfern, and was spending all of her free time in his (less than privileged) neighbourhood. Remember how I told you that it's 'cool to be normal'? This trend applied to boyfriends too. It was proving hard for Tara, who was single and used to having Ebony as her wing woman. At least two mornings a week she'd arrive unannounced at the Queen Bee offices with two takeaway cups of coffee and a box of brunch goodies from Thr1ve cafe (their coconut and almond meal pancakes . . . you will DIE!).

One morning she caught me in the middle of my new daily duty – unpacking Fifi's freebies. Ever since my daughter was born two years ago, baby stores had sent Fifi products to road test, from clothes to baby foods and car seats. They obviously hoped that I'd get them free publicity if I liked them. There really isn't a lot of opportunity for baby products to promote themselves, unless it's in the pages of *My Baby* magazine (and, let's be honest, their readership isn't exactly rolling in money).

You can't even imagine Fifi's daily haul of gifts and goodies. Every morning there was a steady stream of couriers delivering boxes and bags full of tiny outfits and the latest must-have baby gadget. I felt bad asking any of my employees to unpack and sort through the stash, as it wasn't technically Queen Bee business. So I asked Lulu to stack them in the corner of my office and I sorted them into three piles: 'Keep', 'Donate' and 'What the fuck is this?' Seriously, some baby products on the market are downright weird. Fake fringes for babies? A onesie that has a duster attached to the belly so your bub can clean the floor as she crawls? I couldn't even give these away . . .

As Tara leaned back in my reclining desk chair, her long legs stretched out in front of her with her Chloé boots resting on my desk, I confided in her that all these gifts didn't sit well with me. 'I just think it's a bad example to set Fifi,' I complained. 'I want to teach her that nothing in life comes for free – even freebies. All these brands aren't sending this stuff out of the kindness of their hearts, they want publicity.'

Tara picked at the rip in her distressed jeans, looking thoughtful. 'I get what you're saying, Jazz, but you're not begging them to send you freebies. They're doing it because you're semi-famous. Well, you have a profile. And they want you to Insta the shit out of it.'

The problem was I couldn't even post an Instagram photo of most of the products, because some of the brands were competitors of my actual clients. Think about it: I couldn't plug Burberry booties from David Jones on Queen Bee social media when I represented Myer. If this was the olden days I'd just write them a thank-you note and that would be the end of it. But this was 2014, and a pretty card just wouldn't cut it.

'Come on, Tara,' I implored. 'You're always one step ahead of the trend. What's the new-gen etiquette for accepting freebies?'

The blogging maverick, who was now scrolling through Twitter on my computer, looked at me despairingly. 'Well, it's social media, obvs, Jazzy Lou,' she said. 'All these brands want is publicity. They want to know that if they send you one kids' dress they'll make their money back because ten mothers will see it and buy it for their own daughter.'

It was true. When the Duchess of Cambridge had recently visited Sydney with her husband, her one-year-old son had been pictured wearing a kangaroo backpack. Within an hour of the photo going viral, it had sold out. It's a proven fact that shoppers – and mothers in particular – have a lemming mentality. You hook one in and they move en masse.

'It's just a shame Fifi can't write yet,' continued Tara, as she scanned through her Twitterfeed. 'She could have her own Twitter account. How long until she can string together 140-letter sentences, do you think? Any chance you could be raising a child genius?'

She was joking (I think), but actually she'd sparked an idea. My daughter might be too young to write but a picture told a thousand words. That was my light-bulb moment! I could start an Instagram account in Fifi's name, where I posted pictures of the products she genuinely enjoyed. I could pretend it was my two-year-old writing the reviews. Oh, of course people would know it was me, but it would just be a bit of fun.

One of my favourite blogs of recent times was Suri's Burn Book. If you haven't ever read it, then I urge you to do so pronto. It's a sartorial take on the life of Suri Cruise, where the little girl (well, her ghostwriter) critiques the fashion sense of other Hollywood tots. She crushes on Cruz Beckham, hates on Shiloh Jolie-Pitt and is jealous of Beyoncé's child: 'Blue Ivy's vacations are more glamorous than yours. Not more glamorous than mine, because I don't deal with sand or wet grass, but more glamorous than yours.' It's a stroke of genius and has cheered me up on many bad days. If it was written in an adult's voice it wouldn't be nearly as funny, but from the mouths of babes . . . It's so popular the ghostwriter behind the blog now has a book deal.

I was quickly warming to the idea of an Instagram feed for Fifi as a fun side project. My life can be so serious sometimes – all spreadsheets and bottom lines – that this could provide some light relief. And I knew just the person to help me launch my toddler's social media platform. 'ROSA!' I yelled out of my office door. 'Can somebody find me Rosa!'

Within a matter of seconds, my technological whizzkid hot-footed it into my office, carrying an iPhone, an iPad and an Apple Mac laptop and wearing a pair of wireless headphones that looked like they belonged in a sci-fi movie. I'd recently hired the twenty-six-year-old as Queen Bee's social media editor. I needed someone to look after our new blog (after all, I'd be a hypocrite claiming that blogs are the new black if we didn't have one of our own). Rosa was also tasked with looking after our social media channels, digitally courting our Facebook, Instagram, Twitter and Pinterest followers, which was a full-time job in itself.

'Morning, Jasmine!' said Rosa. 'I was actually about to DM you to see if you needed me for anything.' It's a sign of the times when an employee direct messages her boss on Facebook to discuss important work business.

Yet Rosa did things a little differently, which was a trait I admired in her. She had impressed me with her CV, which she'd had screen-printed onto a t-shirt for her application; for our interview she had created a YouTube video which showcased her previous work. The petite redhead had worked in the fashion department of *Dizzy* magazine until it was shut down, along with three other magazines in the portfolio. I felt she needed a lucky break so I hired her.

To welcome my new recruit to the Queen Bee family, I'd flown Rosa to London for a weekend (time is money in the PR world and holidays are speedy). I'd booked her in to attend a one-day web-design seminar called 'How to code in a day'. It was run by an ex-employee of Mark Zuckerberg's. Rosa returned from her trip with an iPhone app she'd designed herself and a long-distance boyfriend (it seemed she'd been the teacher's pet in more ways than one).

'Bud, what are you working on?' I asked as Rosa hovered in my office doorway. 'Actually, whatever it is, forget it and come and sit down.' I turned to Tara, who was looking puzzled, and winked. 'I need you girls to help me on a special project.'

Move over, Suri, because Fifi Lewis, the best-dressed baby and sassiest selfie-poster in Sydney, is about to make her social media debut.

5

Here's a tip: if you're going to bitch about someone over email, make sure the person in question isn't copied in and able to read every word – especially if said person is a valued customer about to spend a quarter of a million dollars with your company.

It all started when I decided to buy myself a new set of wheels to celebrate the ten-year anniversary of Queen Bee launching. Yep, it's already been a decade! Time flies when you're slogging your guts out. Anyway, I know the traditional ten-year anniversary gift is diamonds but, to be frank, I had enough of those already in my collection. Plus, since Fifi had started to walk, the jewellery I wore had got cheaper, as a safety strategy. I was fearful enough wearing my $300,000 engagement ring around my daughter after she toddled off with it one day at the Queen Bee showroom. It took thirty Bees three and a half hours before we found it stuffed in the toe of a Jimmy Choo. That was one risky treasure hunt.

Anyhow, everybody knows that cars are my weakness. When Queen Bee made its first profit, I splashed out $320,000 on a black Aston Martin V8, which was my baby (until my real baby came along and I realised how hard it is to get toddler sick out of cream suede upholstery). Ah well, it was a good excuse to upgrade (and duplicate). Between Michael and me, we have a Mercedes G 63, a Rolls-Royce Phantom and a Bentley. (If any thieves are reading this, our underground car park is extremely secure.)

I also have an Alfa Romeo Giulietta, although it was on loan from a client. All of the Bees were given one, with the Queen Bee logo printed on the doors. I encouraged them to drive around town as much as possible (sorry, planet Earth), and always take a photo of where they parked the car for social media. Here was the Alfa at the shopping centre, outside the gym, on the street near the Park Hyatt. It was like a 'Where's Wally?' but more along the lines of 'Where's the Alfa today?' (You should have seen Rosa's face when I handed her the car keys. When she started working for me, her only mode of transport was a battered second-hand bicycle. That wouldn't do at all!)

I've even started grooming Fifi to follow in my footsteps. When her daddy bought his latest Mercedes G-Class, I ordered an identical miniature version from the United States. It's electronic and comes with every mod con, from heated seats to a DVD player. It even has a personalised number plate, 'F1 F1'. When she parks it in the driveway beside her dad's full-sized version it is utterly adore!

This image was actually one of the first photos I posted to Fifi's Instagram feed when she'd taken her friend Mickey for a spin during a play date:

> Cruising with Mickey in my #Mercedes #gclass. Time to put
> the top down and get some rays in my #Gucci sunnies.

This post got five hundred likes in twenty minutes. It was a winning formula – cars and cute kids! I should actually speak to Mercedes and pitch it to them as an advertising concept.

Anyhow, the car I had in my sights for my anniversary gift-to-self was the new Range Rover Vogue, Supercharged. If I got a sparkly silver paint job it would almost fit into the 'diamond' category, right? I don't believe in bad luck anyway. I make my own luck and strut under ladders just to prove a point. Living on the edge, babe, living on the edge!

'Umm, Jazz, do you really think you need a car designed for off-road driving?' asked Michael when I emailed him a link to my dream vehicle. 'You're not exactly a fan of outdoor pursuits.'

I knew I shouldn't have asked his opinion. And it's not like he was paying for it. I make it a rule never, ever to shop with a man – whether it's for shoes, handbags or motors. Just as Michael didn't understand how I could think harem pants were flattering ('What are you smuggling down there?'), I knew he wouldn't understand my reasons for needing the Range Rover.

Two words — boot space. After struggling to fit my suitcases in my car when I moved into the Four Seasons, I realised I needed more fashion room. A good publicist always keeps at least three changes of ensemble in her car (you never know when your social diary might chuck you a curve ball). I always carried an emergency supply kit in my boot (a YSL little black dress, a Burberry trench and a range of baseball caps for bad hair moments).

I also needed a change of clothes for Fifi, who'd had a little accident when we were driving between appointments with clients last week. That had been another popular Instagram post:

@FifiLewis When you have to go you have to go! I did warn my mum but she wouldn't listen. So I was all soggy — just as well I was organised with a good assortment of ensembles in my bag. Nothing like a highway wardrobe change. #roadtrip #ralphlaurenjeans

I knew all about the Range Rover's four-wheel-drive capabilities (I devour car manuals with the same passion as other women read *Vogue*). And how did Michael know I hadn't suddenly decided to go on an outdoors adventure? I'd actually been thinking about going camping (yes, really, me!). Well, I would obviously glamp more than camp. Did you see Gwyneth Paltrow's recent blog about the 'indoor campsite' in California? They basically pitch a tent in a hotel room, but it's just like being outside because it has forest wallpaper, a fake campfire and these mega-cute metal bunk beds. The tent also has wi-fi and Xboxes to amuse the kids. Note to self – book Michael and me a stay just to prove a point.

I'd gone to my usual car showroom to test drive the Range Rover (the owner of the showroom had just bought a $8.7 million mansion in Watsons Bay, which I swear I mostly financed with my repeat business over the years). When I put down my order I paid the deposit in cash. This is my tradition when buying a car. In a weird way it adds to the buzz, handing over an envelope as thick as a brick, stuffed with notes. I earned it, why not get a power kick from spending it? Oh, but wait – was that the newest-model Bentley in the corner? I didn't even know the Flying Spur was available in Australia yet . . . Come on, Jazzy Lou, control yourself – a $280,000 purchase is enough for one morning.

It took all my self-discipline to drag myself out of the showroom without a second set of car keys. Afterwards I just couldn't stop thinking about those leopard-like curves and leather interior. I felt lovesick as I sat in my office, and had no appetite to eat the superfood salad that Lulu had gone all the way to Bondi to fetch from the new Paleo Cafe.

Could I buy two cars in one day? Would Michael kill me? In my opinion it was no different to buying two bras in one shopping trip. You can go years without finding one that is the perfect fit for you, so when you do, buy in bulk! It's an investment.

The deciding moment came when I clicked onto the *Daily Mail* website. The first photograph that flashed onto my computer screen was of Kim Kardashian stepping out of the Flying Spur. The reality television star was stepping out of MY car. It was a sign from the universe that I had to have one.

Feeling slightly giddy with adrenaline, I fired off an email to the showroom's manager Richard Smeedon:

> Hi Richard. Long time no see (LOLZ). I'd love to test drive the new Bentley you have in the showroom please. Can you organise for one to be brought to my offices as soon as possible?

Within a matter of minutes I'd received a reply. I was such a valued customer, this guy probably had a special alert for my emails, which played 'Big Spender' every time I sent a message.

> From: RSmeedon@Wheelspin.com
> To: Jasmine@Queenbee.com
> Hi Jasmine,
> Of course! More than happy to arrange. I've cc'ed in my colleague Adam Peterson who will organise this pronto.
> Warm regards,   ,
> Richard

All sorted, all very easy, all very amicable – until Adam entered the email conversation:

From: APeterson@Wheelspin.com

To: RSmeedon@Wheelspin.com

CC: Jasmine@Queenbee.com

Seriously, is this a publicity stunt? She's just bought a Range
Rover and now she wants a Bentley too? Come on!!!!!

(Sent from my iPhone)

I bet Adam was typing on the move, probably while driving. Maybe that's why he didn't notice that I was still copied into the conversation and could read every word of his slur. Dumb arse.

I nearly choked on my sparkling water when I read it. I imagine Richard had the same reaction, as my mobile immediately began to ring, flashing up his office number. Oh no, Richie; I knew better than to speak to him on the phone when I wanted every word of our exchange down in writing.

To: RSmeedon@Wheelspin.com

CC: APeterson@Wheelspin.com

From: Jasmine@Queenbee.com

Hi all,

In light of the below email exchange I will take up my right of
the cooling-off period in regards to the Range Rover order, and
would appreciate it if you could refund my deposit immediately.
I will be taking my order to another dealer who exercises
some professionalism. Richard, I'll await your confirmation of
cancellation and refund of the deposit.

If publicity is what you want then publicity is what I'll get you . . . but it won't necessarily be the kind you're after. The newspapers will love the email below, I have no doubt.

To quote your employee, 'Come on!'

I then forwarded the email exchange to Michael. It's not that I need a man to fight my battles, but I did secretly hope it would awake his inner white knight and make him jump to my defence – which it did.

To: RSmeedon@Wheelspin.com
CC: Jasmine@Queenbee.com
From: Michaellloyd@gmail.com
Interesting way to treat potential clients . . . Oh and by the way, so, so, so many of my friends and family are clients of yours. Can't wait to ruin your day . . .
Regards,
Your former customer

I did a little air punch when I read Michael's email. Way to hit them where it hurt – right in their annual profit! From here there was a flurry of emails from Richard and Adam. How I'd love to be a fly on the wall in their showroom. This from Adam:

My previous email was genuinely not meant in the way that it reads. As I hope you would agree, emails and text messages are written so quickly and can easily be taken out of context.

This was followed by several 'I'm sorry, Jasmine' emails. Yawn, yawn! I would have been far more forgiving if he'd stood by his insult, but trying to backtrack and say that I'd taken it out of context only enraged me more.

But here's where it really gets interesting. A week later (by which time I'd taken my order for both cars to a rival dealer), I received an email from Luke. Subject line: 'What have you got yourself into this time? LOLZ'. Luke had forwarded me an email he'd been sent by a woman called Hattie Peterson. Hang on, I recognised that surname. It turned out to be the wife of my new enemy Adam 'Is this a publicity stunt?' Peterson.

Dear Luke,

I am writing with a story that I think will interest you, involving publicist Jasmine Lewis and an employer called Adam Peterson at Wheel Spin motors. I have included below an email exchange between them. It should be self-explanatory.

How did I get these emails? Well, I happen to be the estranged wife of the dumb-arse car dealer who is now trying to run me out of town. I have a restraining order out against him and I am currently in hiding with our two-year-old son (but I still know the password to his email account). He is threatening to report me to the police for robbery, if I don't give him back the car he bought me for my last birthday. He also refuses to pay maintenance, despite the fact that he earns more than $400k a year and drives a bright yellow GTC.

I hope this story gets out so people can see the true mark of the man!

Do what you like with these emails, just please don't mention that they came from me.

Sincerely,
Hattie Peterson

I couldn't believe it! It seemed that I'd got off lightly compared to some of the other women in Adam's life. For a moment I considered telling Luke to run the story. However, I'm all too aware there are always two sides to every relationship breakdown (if you listened to Belle Single I was a Jezebel for stealing Michael from her), so even though he was itching to run it, I told Luke to let this one go. I had to bribe him by promising to get gossip on Leonardo DiCaprio, who had just moved into the Four Seasons' penthouse suite. I'd overheard the cleaners discussing some very interesting items they'd found in his bathroom . . .

I really didn't want to be a pawn in a divorce – especially when it sounded sooo messy. Suddenly I felt very thankful for my own relationship. We may feel like we live on different planets sometimes, but at least Michael came to my rescue when I needed him.

6

'Jazzy Lou, I have Foxy on line one,' called Lulu from the reception desk. 'She wants to know if you can decorate her whole apartment – gratis!'

It was a good thing Lulu had put the Australian model on hold so that she didn't hear my cry of despair. Seriously! Why do my clients think I'm some freaking fairy godmother?

It had been six months since I launched The Talent Hive, and the rollover had been slightly more stressful than I anticipated. This was partly because I hadn't culled my other clients as quickly as I planned, so I was basically still running my old business alongside my new business. It was cray-cray!

Why hadn't I dumped the clients on my hit list? Well, a lot of them – when they got a sniff of rejection – just got sooo needy. They were sending flowers and cupcakes and, more importantly, suddenly upping their rates. ('You're worth it, Jasmine. We don't want you to feel underappreciated.') I was being corporately courted and actually quite enjoying it. Call me a sucker – or call me a savvy businesswoman – but I planned to string them along for a little bit longer. That did mean, however, that the Bees and I were doing double the workload to manage our old clients plus the new blogging dynasty. Working 9 to 5? I now worked 24/7.

It didn't help that some of the bloggers were proving to be . . . difficult. When I'd decided to focus on creatives, I thought it would be a doddle compared to handling the diva fashion designers and corporate honchos with huge egos, but I was finding that managing bloggers could be even more of a challenge.

This latest phone call from Foxy was a case in point. She wasn't even a bona fide blogger really, but fell into the category of 'social media personality' because she has 130,000 Instagram followers and a further 180,000 on Facebook. The model had been an unknown on the circuit for years, shooting ad campaigns for toothpaste and cystitis remedies. Then, during last year's Sydney Fashion Week, she got her lucky break. Not on the runway (no designer at that point knew her name) but at an after-party. She had somehow blagged her way into the *Bizarre* magazine party at the QT Hotel and found herself sharing a disabled toilet with Cara Delevingne, who'd been flown over by Topshop for their catwalk show. The paparazzi caught them leaving the nightclub arm in drunken arm, and started a 'who's that girl?' hunt. Suddenly, everyone wanted a piece of Foxy. And didn't she just revel in it . . .

On Instagram she was a cute girl-next-door, posting photos of her leopard-print bed socks, her favourite coffee mug and the flowers she'd bought for her mother. Every girl on the street wanted to be her. Unfortunately, she didn't come with a personality filter in the real world. She was a spoilt brat and a prolific name dropper. At our first meeting she also scolded me for ordering a coffee ('Think of your adrenal glands, Jasmine'), before taking her green smoothie outside so she could light up a Marlboro Menthol.

Yet there were many benefits in managing Foxy. It was very easy to get her work, as she was currently the flavour of the fashion world. Even Victoria's Secret were interested in Foxy wearing their famous diamond bra at their next show. So it was worth me playing nice and putting up with her diva-isms (although some mornings it was easier than others). As I picked up the phone, to one of my most profitable clients, I braced myself for today's outlandish request.

'Jazzy Lou! Foxy here,' my client cried down the line at her usual hundred decibels. 'I've got some *reaaaally* exciting news! You might have read in *The Sun* that I've just bought a new apartment. It's a cute little place on the hill above Icebergs. In the same block as the pad where Belle Single used to film her reality show . . . although my apartment is double the size of that cow's.'

I tried not to laugh down the phone – it was no secret that Foxy and Belle were arch enemies on the modelling circuit ever since they'd competed for the same *Playboy* cover (neither of them got it). Foxy's hatred of Michael's ex-girlfriend may have been another reason I was happy to represent her (I know, unprofessional, but I'm only human and every now and again my emotions get the better of me).

'I did read about your new pad. It sounds beyond,' I told Foxy. 'I saw the at-home photo shoot you did for *Bizarre* magazine too. That carpet, those paintings! You did an incredible job on the home decorating. Who's your interior designer?'

Foxy let out a laugh. 'Oh, that? All of that was borrowed for the photo shoot – the magazine styled it for me and then took it all away when they were done. My new pad is just a big white box right now. I don't own anything. In fact, that's why I'm calling . . . I'm lacking a few teeny tiny bits and pieces to make it homely. Okay, I'm missing a shitload. And I know you're a bit of an interiors expert . . .'

Suddenly I knew exactly where this conversation was going. When I'd last bumped into Foxy, at the unveiling of the new Chanel store in Sydney, I had mentioned that I was currently in the midst of an interiors overhaul and that I'd found the perfect dressing table on a super-cute website called Home Economics, which was owned by a girl I went to high school with. I was just making small talk and didn't even think Foxy was listening, but I'd clearly underestimated the strength of her shopping addiction.

'So, Jazz, I've been looking on that website you were telling me about,' trilled Foxy. 'There are *sooo* many awesome things on there. I'm having a *Desperate Housewives* moment! Could I possibly send you a list of the items I'd just *lurrrve* for my new place? I remember you said you're friends with the owner and I know how persuasive you are . . .'

Why is it that the more money people make the less they want to pay for? It must be an affliction that occurs when your income hits six figures.

'I'm delighted you like the range so much,' I schmoozed Foxy, trying to buy time while I thought of a polite way to refuse. 'The thing is, my friend has only just launched the company so I don't know if she's in a position to give anything away. It depends on the "essentials" you're looking for, I suppose. What's on your wish list?'

'Do you mean in an ideal world?' asked Foxy. 'I'd like 10,000 sets of 10,000-count Egyptian-cotton sheets, and a new latex pillow for every night. I'd also like to never wash a pot or pan again, so a daily supply would be awesome . . . only joking . . . well, kind of. Hahahahahahahahahahahaha.'

The model laughed for far longer than felt natural or comfortable. Oh Foxy, you're so funny . . . not. I bet she'd carefully practised that joke before calling me so that when she made her 'real' demands (which were probably only fraction-ally less excessive), they would seem modest in comparison. It was the oldest trick in the book.

'Why don't you email me links to *one* or *two* products you'd like?' I told her with careful emphasis. 'Although I have to warn you, I know they're short on stock at the moment so they might not have much available. I know they'd LOVE to help you if only they had more stock in their warehouse.'

This was another trick I'd learned early in my career as a publicist: if in doubt, pull the 'out of stock' excuse. It wasn't worth the possible fallout if you told a celebrity that a brand hadn't heard of them – or didn't care about them enough to cough up some free stuff.

As expected, when Foxy sent over her wish list, it would have made Kim Kardashian's gift registry look modest: a Smeg fridge in peppermint green, a limited-edition Shepard Fairey print, and a $6000 gold and marble Versace coffee table. I realised I shouldn't have told Foxy to email the list over, as I bet if she'd had to read it out to me over the phone – or tell me face to face – she'd have been too embarrassed to ask for so much.

As I read Foxy's email I thought about life before social media, when celebrities had less to bargain with. Back then, for a celeb to be given a free product they would have to guarantee they'd be snapped by a newspaper wearing it, but now, thanks to the selfie, everyone was their own pap.

'I really appreciate this, Jazzy Lou,' wrote Foxy. 'If you need any photos of me lounging on my new sofa for Home Economics' Insta feed then just let me know. I'm happy to oblige! You're a total lifesaver organising all of this. You'll have to come over for dinner once my new things arrive.'

A lifesaver? I wasn't convinced that Foxy's life would be at risk if she couldn't sit her perfectly pert bottom on a Missoni cashmere sofa cushion. But maybe she had an unusual terminal illness I'd never heard of that could only be cured by high-end upholstery.

What really grated was the fact that she could easily have afforded to buy the goodies herself. As was the case with many fashion bloggers, Foxy's parents were loaded. Even before her modelling career took off, she was the smug owner of a Hermès Birkin bag. So what? Well, only twenty-four of these bags were ever created – each one was crafted from material taken from crocodile skin and cost $45,000 a pop. So, yes, Foxy could probably afford to furnish her own flat. And not just from Ikea. Yet she was far from the first high-profiler to think that paying for home decor was beneath her.

Before launching The Talent Hive, I had heard rumours about certain bloggers and how their newfound fame was inflating their egos. I had hoped the stories were exaggerated and that the people spreading them were just jealous of their success. Could a bunch of amateur writers really be divas? After only a few weeks working with them, I could say a resounding yes.

I blame BryanBoy, the most famous fashion blogger on the circuit, and a judge on *America's Next Top Model*. Back in 2010, BryanBoy (real name Bryan Grey Yambao) boasted that he made $100,000 a year from blogging, and his salary can only have skyrocketed since then. He'd even had a Marc Jacobs handbag named after him (the ultimate honour). 'I love your passion for fashion,' said Jacobs. 'Where would designers be without enthusiasm like yours?'

How do bloggers make their moolah? Well, selling advertising space on their website is the most obvious means, but bloggers with big profiles also have additional revenue streams. The numbers may shock you: for between $5000 and $20,000 a brand can hire a blogger to host an event (they also need to cover the cost of travel, hotel and food, naturally); and then there's Fashion Week, where designers are reported to pay bloggers up to $10,000 to sit front row at their shows, pushing the celebrities and fashion editors to the cheap seats at the back.

These superstar bloggers would argue that it's their full-time job and therefore they should be paid handsomely. I'd recently read an interview with BryanBoy in which he moaned: 'Fashion Month is a huge business expense for me.' You know, what with all the outfits to buy, the champagne to swig, the first-class flights to take. During Fashion Weeks, BryanBoy rents three-bedroom apartments in Milan and Paris, and splits the cost with fellow blogger Rumi Neely from Fashion Toast. 'This way we have tons of space, a living area, fast internet and room for our assistant.'

If I sound bitter, it's only because I wasn't given anything for free when I was clawing my way up the ranks. I attended my first London Fashion Week when I was twenty-three years old, working as a dogsbody at Wilderstein PR, my first publicity job.

I was only allowed to go at all because my boss from hell, Diane Wilderstein, had fired her assistant a few days before and needed someone to carry her handbag. I was out-of-my-mind excited, especially as I knew Diane always stayed at the very exclusive Landmark Hotel in Piccadilly. I was only told when I arrived in Heathrow that she'd actually booked me a bunk bed in a dormitory in a hostel in Camden (I flew back to Sydney with a suitcase full of Topshop and a severe case of bed bugs).

This incident was proof that bosses should be careful how they treat their minions, as once they've matured you may need them – or at least not want them as your enemy. When I first launched Queen Bee, many of Wilderstein PR's clients had defected to me, kickstarting a lengthy, bitter rivalry, which I didn't exactly discourage.

When I was pregnant with Fifi I had briefly considered selling Queen Bee PR to a Russian investor called Ivan Shavalik – until I discovered that his business practices weren't exactly kosher. It turned out the cashed-up businessman was being investigated by immigration officials for entering Australia illegally, and some of his other business deals were more 'backstreet' than boardroom.

Okay, maybe it wasn't fair of me to palm Ivan off onto Diane, but really it was her fault for putting her jealousy before her business sense. When Diane heard I'd torn up my contract with the Russians, she saw it as an opportunity to one-up me and approached Ivan to invest in her company instead. Did it end well? What do you think? The last I heard, Ivan was in jail for fraud and Diane was in a rehabilitation facility in Far North Queensland having suffered a nervous breakdown. She may have been my business rival, but even I wished her well.

My career had certainly not been all plain sailing; however, it was all part of my induction into PR and I could now proudly look back and say I'd survived the struggles. This wasn't the case for many bloggers, who seemed to have skipped the 'growing pains' period and jumped straight from unknowns to somebodies.

In fact, one of my newest sign-ups, a fashion blogger by the name of Savannah Jagger (blog name Dare to Ware), has three assistants (yes, three!) who follow her absolutely everywhere. 'I need one to carry my camera, one to carry my suitcase of gear and the other to handle my admin,' she told me. 'I also need all three to sort through the free gifts that I'm sent. You have no idea, Jazzy Lou – it was getting so stressful unpacking everything myself.'

Remember when I said earlier how fashion editors are being starved of free gifts? I blamed the recession for the fact that brands apparently no longer have money to chuck around presents. However, it seems I was wrong – the freebies have just been reallocated. If the fashion editors of *Bizarre* and *Eve Pascal* want to know why last year Gucci gave them a free handbag for Christmas and this year they were given a key ring, just look on the arm of Nicole Warne from Gary Pepper or Jessica Stein from Tuula. That's where your freebies have gone!

Just for the record, this isn't true for all bloggers. For every blogger who's sitting on a gold mine, there are a hundred working for rocks (and I don't mean the shiny ten-carat kind). The majority of the bloggers overloading the web are making absolute nada from their online style diaries: no advertising, no freebies, no invitations to Fashion Week.

The real internet superstars apparently have the opposite problem. What is the etiquette when you're sent more free clothes than you have time to wear, let alone blog about?

'It's *sooo* tough,' moaned Savannah during our first meeting. 'I don't know how all these fashion houses and PR companies get my address, but they won't stop sending me clothes, shoes, handbags, everything! Then they expect me to use my profile to get them attention. I'm going insane here, Jazzy Lou, trying to decide what to write about and what not to.'

The fashion blogger had arrived at the Queen Bee offices trailed by her assistants, who were wearing matching uniforms of black Acne Studios trousers and plain white J.Crew t-shirts. Their clothes were a stark contrast to Savannah's racy outfit – a leopard-print maxi skirt with a split up to her knicker line and a white blazer fastened with one button. I can only assume she didn't want to risk being outshone, so ordered her assistants to dress in sensible monochrome.

'Hmm, all those free gifts do sound stressful,' I said, struggling to look sympathetic. 'If you want I could send out a press release to everyone in the fashion industry stating that you no longer want to receive freebies of any kind as it's damaging to your artistic integrity.'

I had been half joking, but in fact this was a pretty neat idea. Recently bloggers were getting a lot of criticism for being paid to write positive reviews about products. This could be a great publicity stunt and a unique selling point for Savannah:

The blogger who can't be bought; the stylista who isn't a sellout. It could be the new version of 'models who don't wear makeup'. I bet *Style* magazine would be up for an interview on the topic. In my head, I already had a five-point plan for the concept, but then I noticed that Savannah's face looked like thunder.

'Will you shut the fuck up, Jasmine?' she hissed, as if the fashion industry had bugged my office. 'I didn't say I don't want freebies. I just said I only wanted the good gifts. How do you think I can afford to look this stylish if I don't get my clothes for free? I'm not made of money, you know. I have seven credit cards. SEVEN! My daddy will only give me a $2000 a month clothing allowance. I NEED free gifts. I've EARNED free gifts . . . I just need you to act as a gatekeeper so that I'm not sent tat from last season. It BORES me.'

I didn't think that press release would be quite as snappy: 'Please note that Savannah Jagger will only be accepting gifts that match her style standards. Please do not send any vertical stripes or synthetic fabrics, and do not, under any circumstances, send any item from last season.'

I'm not judging. How could I? I like the finer things in life, too, although I haven't always been able to afford them. In the earlier stages of my career, when I was a twenty-three-year-old PR flunky on a limited budget, I would beg, borrow and steal to get the latest It bag. I bought my first Birkin by pawning a necklace I was given for my twenty-first birthday. That's not as bad as the guy who sold his kidney to buy his girlfriend the Hermès Grace Kelly bag (true story).

I would also be a hypocrite to judge these blogger-blaggers when my own daughter's wardrobe is made up of freebies and clothes bought with a generous discount. As BryanBoy recently tweeted: 'A diva is just the female version of a hustler.' If that is the case, then game on!

7

Whenever I told people that we were living in a hotel they always gasped in envy, but it did have its drawbacks. The most significant issue was the lack of space. The novelty of our room had soon worn off. Suite? It was more like a bedsit with a living area and two bedrooms. I'd even considered upgrading to a mezzanine suite, but Fifi was walking and the stairs didn't come with childproof gates. Oh, life was much simpler when I was a single twenty-something-year-old (not that I could have afforded to stay in a place like this then).

I hated to sound ungrateful so I tried to make the most of it. There were many, many perks to being a long-term hotel guest (no cleaning, room service on call, fresh bed sheets every day if I wanted them), and Fifi and I soon got into the rhythm of living in the Four Seasons.

Every morning, after our 5 am wakeup call from reception, I'd find a tray outside my door with my morning drinks order: a double espresso made with the hotel's unique blend of coffee beans, and a babyccino for my mini me.

After our caffeine or dairy hit we'd choose our outfits for the day. Fifi was going through a stage where she insisted that we colour-coordinate. 'Matchy match, Mummy!' she'd scream. Luckily, a lot of designers had had the same idea this season and had created junior versions of their adult outfits. Our current favourite was a checked Victoria Beckham dress with a Peter Pan collar. It was age-appropriate for the both of us (although goddamn Fifi for looking better in it than me).

I've always put a lot of effort into Fifi's ensembles. In my opinion you're never too young to dress to impress. Plus I enjoyed being imaginative with her look. The best thing about having a daughter is being able to dress her in the fashion I was too ancient to get away with (Carrie's tutu from *Sex in the City*, Blair's pussy bows from *Gossip Girl*).

I had even more motivation to up Fifi's style game since her Instagram feed had taken off with a vengeance. I couldn't believe it when, within five months of me creating the account, my daughter had 60,000 Instagram followers. Way to go, girl! I'm not sure how her profile had grown so rapidly, or so internationally. Some of her followers were my friends, colleagues and acquaintances, but many were strangers from every corner of the globe. Fifi had her own unique fan base: parents who genuinely wanted recommendations on baby products, and voyeurs who were just intrigued by her extravagant lifestyle.

At the beginning it was mainly pictures of Fifi's 'outfit of the day' with a funny commentary: 'Every girl needs a tennis bracelet and a Kenzo frock, right?' or 'A little leopard print always has a place in my wardrobe.' However, her freebies didn't end at clothes; there were beauty products and kiddies' foods to road-test.

It was like a cartoon strip of Fifi's lifestyle, which does seem lavish compared to the average pre-schooler's existence. Wherever I go, Fifi goes. She is my best friend, after all – why wouldn't I want her with me? An average day might start with a hair appointment, then on to a press breakfast held on a yacht in the harbour, then to lunch at the Park Hyatt, a fashion photo shoot in the afternoon and dinner at Rick Stein's restaurant (Fifi loves the soufflé). She had her own social commitments too: baby yoga, swimming class and invitations to the premieres of kids' movies. I also made sure I posted photos of her downtime: Fifi flicking through a fashion magazine, playing on her iPad or having a manicure. None of these were staged; this is really how she spends her time.

I was even a bit jealous of her popularity, if I'm honest. It had taken me years to build up Queen Bee's 70,000 Instagram followers, even with the help of a full-time social media assistant. Now, practically overnight, my daughter had captured the hearts of the internet. I needed more friends in my life. She could give me some pointers.

'I'm having so much fun ghostwriting Fifi's posts,' I told Shelley when she popped by the office to drop off a Herve Léger skirt which had clearly 'shrunk in the mail'. I was really hitting my stride with my tongue-in-cheek posts, if I do say so myself (especially after a few Marshmellow cocktails at The Den).

'Oh my god, I am OBSESSED with your child,' crowed Shelley, who is Fifi's godmother so probably a little biased. 'Her Instagram account is like a fly-on-the-wall reality TV show. There was one post the other week which had me in stitches . . .' She pulled out her iPhone in its Hermès carry case and jabbed her finger at the touch screen. When she found the post in question, she turned the screen in my direction. Ah, yes, I'd been particularly happy with that one:

Trying out a new body cream today. I need to keep this skin supple as long as possible. I don't want to end up all leathery like Mum. #kiehls #babybodylotion #verynice

I was having great fun taking the piss out of myself in Fifi's posts (I did tell you self-deprecation is the key to being likeable). I never pretend to be perfect and I'm happy to make light of my flaws. Later the same day, I'd taken a snapshot of my daughter flipping little plastic burgers on her toy barbecue:

At least somebody can cook in this household. My mum is not exactly a domestic goddess. #childlabour

It's no wonder, really, that people found her so intriguing. Although the feedback wasn't all positive, and some of Fifi's Instagram followers seemed to love to hate her. Well, they loved to hate me. None of the trolling was aimed at Fifi directly. They accepted she wasn't a bad kid. I was just a bad mother.

The most common criticism was aimed at my poor spelling. Yes, I was under attack from the punctuation police, and my latest crime against the English language was this post from Fifi:

This freakin weather is totally affecting my mojo. New jeans @jbrandjeans and my sequin @sperrytopsider boat shoes.

Within three minutes of my posting the photo, a troll was on my case for dropping the 'g' from 'freaking'. Seriously, people! Apparently I was setting a terrible example, not only for my daughter but for children everywhere. And did I not know how to use spellcheck?

When I read the comment my initial response was, 'Get a life, woman.' I have never, ever pretended to be book smart (what I lack in academic knowledge I make up for in bloodyminded determination). But should I retort or ignore? Stoke the fire or let it die? As I sat at my desk, pondering my options, I noticed that the post already had twenty-seven comments beneath it. Groan! Who else was going to attack my IQ? But it seems that Fifi's fans are loyal – both to my daughter and to me – and were jumping to our defence. I soon found that if anything negative was posted under Fifi's picture, I didn't need to fight back, as the Insta-sphere would do the dirty work for me:

Well, if the spelling mistakes bother you so much just don't follow @Fifilewis. You are not Jazzy Lou's teacher so just back off. Don't worry, Fifi and Jasmine, the world is full of nasty people who have nothing better to do than troll.

Great businesswomen can be shit spellers. It's probably because we are not afraid to make mistakes and do not fixate on them when we do.

Look at how successful you are @queenbeepr. You're famous and a millionaire. It looks like spelling hasn't gotten in your way!

Still, the negative feedback didn't end at my spelling; people were also quick to judge my parenting skills, which apparently they could assess based on one daily snapshot. For the record, I do not pretend to be a perfect mother. When Fifi was born I didn't have a clue what I was doing, and two years on I felt just as ignorant. But fake it till you make it – I do the best I can.

Plus, at the moment I was practically a single mother, seeing as Michael could only manage a once-a-week visit (something about the economic climate, and his bank possibly folding. Whatever). Okay, I have a nanny – an amazing English girl called Alice who not only knows the words to every Wiggles song but also used to be a window dresser at Louis Vuitton (before she realised that nannying added an extra zero onto her salary). The other day I came home to find that Alice and

Fifi had built a perfect replica of a Vuitton handbag out of Lego. Needless to say, I adore her! But I do like to limit her hours as much as possible so I can be a hands-on mother.

You'd think I'd get brownie points for preferring to bond with my daughter than leave her with a hired carer, but it seemed I couldn't win. If I left Fifi with a nanny I was deserting her; if I included her in my schedule I was overtaxing her.

Early one morning, I'd posted a photograph of Fifi and myself, both looking tired and puffy-faced as we sipped on green juices in my office:

> What else does one do at 5 am other than selfies with my mama? Burning the candle at both ends while we work on an exciting project. #workaholics

It was cute – even if the photo of me was extremely unflattering. (Note to self: must book Botox appointment.) I certainly didn't expect the torrent of abuse it caused. Apparently, I was putting my child's health at risk by making her get up so early. Some people wrongly assumed we hadn't yet gone to bed. I can understand it might have looked that way, but as if I'd pull an all-nighter with a toddler!

I bit my tongue. Let my Insta-fans and my Insta-foes fight it out:

> People, get off her back. You don't know her. She is clearly a great mum and obviously you've forgotten that toddlers wake up at 5 am without any help. I'm sure she is getting enough

rest. Good work @QueenBeepr — you're an inspiration to a lot of women.

I have a rule never to delete any negative posts left on Fifi's page. I have nothing to hide, and it's not like my daughter is old enough to read them, although she does love flicking through the photos and is quite capable of grabbing my iPhone, inputting the passcode and clicking open Instagram herself.

The biggest backlash came when I posted a photo of Fifi wearing a bikini during a day out on Bondi Beach. The irony is that it's my absolute favourite Fifi snapshot. She was wearing an American baseball cap with 'Slugger' stamped across the rim and pulling a pose like a rapper. The bikini is Ralph Lauren, printed with the stars and stripes of the American flag. A lot of her Instagram followers loved it ('This tot has serious 'tude'). That photo scored 589 likes and 270 comments, but they weren't all complimentary:

> You should be ashamed of yourself @queenbeepr for over-sexualisation of your daughter. Why don't you just get her a stripper pole? #toomuchtoosoon

Too provocative for a two-year-old? Oh, pleeease. If you go to Bondi Beach on any day you'll see hundreds of two-year-olds running around with nothing on. At least Fifi was wearing a cossie — even if it had high-cut bottoms and a triangle bra.

I also took offence at the accusations that I was a pushy parent, as some trolls suggested. I am not some fame-starved stage mother who wants her daughter to be in the spotlight, and I wasn't forcing Fifi into these photo shoots. In fact, I had to rein in her posing. This kid could give Kate Moss a run for her money.

I'm naturally very camera shy, although I've learned to hide it as I spend so much of my time at fashion shoots and in TV studios. But Fifi hadn't inherited my self-conscious streak. The moment I pulled out my iPhone – even if it was just to make a phone call – she saw it as her 'moment': 'Mummy, flash me! Mummy, photo,' she'd yell, which could be very inconvenient when we were in a public place.

What's more, she'd also started doing an exaggerated pout. Imagine Janice Dickinson – and quadruple it. I have to accept responsibility for this one, as I know Fifi picked it up from me. During a recent photo shoot for *Style* magazine, I'd been messing around with the makeup artist, taking the piss out of the rich women in my neighbourhood who have overdone the injectables (we call them the 'Double Bay lips'). Fifi must have been watching and decided it would be her signature facial expression. She now refused to smile in any photograph, no matter how much I tried to coax her. It reminded me of a piece of advice I'd been given by Brit designer Henry Holland: he mouths the word 'prune' instead of 'cheese' in photos as he says it makes for a more flattering lip shape. For Fifi, it was the pout or nothing.

This new look was pretty embarrassing when we posed for a family photo at her grandmother's eighty-fifth birthday party and there at the front was this little redhaired two-year-old plumping her lips like a Playboy bunny. That wasn't one for the mantelpiece. I'm sure Fifi will grow out of it (maybe, hopefully), and the plus side is that her fans adore it.

It was Rosa who suggested we make a hashtag for #thelipsthelips to see if we could start it trending. I was becoming a little insecure about my Instagram posts since the trolls had started lurking, so had I had asked the Queen Bee tech expert to vet every photo and comment before I made it public. 'It could become a thing,' said Rosa excitedly. 'Just like Angelina's leg after the Oscars.'

Hmm, that wouldn't be a bad social experiment – finding out how easy it was to start a viral trend. So the next time Fifi pulled out her pout, as we tucked into sushi in bed one night, I decided to test out the hashtag:

Dinner time! Giving the tuna a run for its money with my fish lips. #thelipsthelips

It was a popular picture – 310 likes in three minutes – but would the hashtag go viral? Hell yes! A week later, when Rosa showed me how to search for hashtags, we discovered there were photos of people copying Fifi's pose from all around the world. There were people doing #thelipsthelips from here to China. I couldn't believe it had taken off so fast, but that's the power of social media.

Until this experiment I'd still seen Instagram as a light-hearted hobby, but big brands clearly saw it as a commercial opportunity. Even the backlash only got Fifi more attention – no publicity is bad publicity.

Ever since Fifi made her online debut, my tot had been sent more free gifts than ever. It was getting a little ridiculous, especially as many were couriered directly to the hotel rather than my office. The Four Seasons staff had actually dedicated an area of the post room to Fifi's haul so that I didn't need to clutter our suite with glittery boxes and bubble-gum pink bags (I wish kiddies' ranges would choose a less stereotypical colour scheme for their packaging).

I had a rule not to promote a product unless Fifi genuinely liked it, whether that was clothes, snacks or car seats. A new range of frilly socks got the thumbs-up and made it onto Instagram, but others weren't so lucky. She turned her nose up at a new range of glittery jelly shoes ('No, Mummy. Silly, Mummy!'), and did a little pretend vomit after trying a new brand of wheatgrass-flavoured yoghurts. I think Anna Wintour has a similar reaction to fashion shows she isn't impressed by.

If a product didn't pass Fifi's litmus test then I wouldn't photograph it. I never wrote negative reviews on her Instagram page – if a product wasn't good I just wouldn't say anything at all.

I tried to explain this to the marketing manager of Jolly Juice when she called (for the sixth time in three days) to ask when they might see their product on Fifi's Instagram feed.

'The thing is, Carla, I didn't actually request the free samples,' I replied firmly, 'therefore we're under no obligation to give you publicity. I hate to say this, but Fifi just didn't like them and she has a responsibility to her fans to tell the truth. A lot of mothers and children rely on her advice. Do you want me to turn my daughter into a liar?'

This was the moment I learned the pulling power of Brand Fifi. There was a pause on the other end of the line, and then Carla said in a hushed voice, 'What if we make it worth your while? We can pay for one post of Fifi raving about our product . . . how does $300 for one post sound?'

I knew, of course, that many fashion bloggers are paid to promote products on social media. A subtle bit of product placement could earn a blogger a big payday. Yet I really hadn't considered that brands would offer the same deal for a toddler. Was this stepping over the line?

'That's a very generous offer from Jolly Juice,' I said. 'Can I get back to you? I'll have to check with Fifi's management team.'

I was bluffing, of course. What I really meant was, 'I'll have to check with her father.' I had told Michael about Fifi's Instagram account during our weekly email update, and he'd 'LOLed' back but hadn't really seemed interested. Before taking Fifi's brand to the next level, however, I felt like I should consult him. I tried to call his mobile but there was no answer. I tried Viber, Facetime and Skype but all rang out. Why could I never get hold of my husband when I needed him?

The thing with business is that there's often only a small window of opportunity. And so I made a decision – I would take the $300, just this once. I would use it to pay for Fifi's next set of yoga classes.

I really did intend to leave it at that one deal, but the following week the same marketing manager called to say her firm was delighted with the boost in sales they'd seen after the post went up, and would I take $300 a post to promote some of their other products?

Okay, I'm a mother first, but I'm also a businesswoman, and I'd be a failure at both if I let this opportunity pass. I want to teach Fifi the value of money and for her to have success in her own right. The blogging bubble would soon burst, but for now I should leverage its potential. Like any mother, I spend my days taking photos of my adorable daughter anyway – why shouldn't she get paid for it? If I could make Fifi's Instagram feed a commercial reality, well, lucky her. I could put any cash she made straight into her bank account and when she's older she'll have a little nest egg (on top of her trust fund, obviously).

My motto when it comes to business is 'consider, assess, action'. Well, I'd considered my options and made my decision. By the end of the day, Fifi's photograph had been added to The Talent Hive's website, with a breakdown of her fees for sponsored posts and public appearances. If I was going to launch my daughter's brand I would do it properly.

When most toddlers pout it's a temper tantrum – when Fifi pouts it gets hundreds of Instagram likes. With a bevy of brands at her disposal, a wardrobe coveted by fashionistas and a razor-sharp wit, Fifi's digital presence is irresistible. Fifi has an uncanny ability to elevate a brand simply by association and knows how to mix budget and luxury products with ease – who else wears Gucci sandals one day and Crocs the next? She's the voice of a generation.

And so I launched my daughter's career – before she was even old enough to pronounce the words 'alter ego'. From that moment on, she wasn't just Fifi Lewis – she was the 'pint-sized Instagrammer' and the 'two-year-old tastemaker'.

Umm . . . I may have a created a monster.

8

So it turned out all I needed to do to get my husband's attention was 'sell out' our daughter. Well, that was what my critics accused me of. Michael hadn't even noticed that I'd added Fifi to The Talent Hive's website, until the *Australian Women's Weekly* published a story on Fifi. They dubbed her the 'millionaire Insta-tot' and printed her rate card, showing that she charged a minimum of $200 for a sponsored post.

I then received a call from Freya Harrison, an ex-magazine editor turned mummy blogger, who could give Perez Hilton a run for his money when it came to cattiness. 'Jazzy Lou, darling, we're writing an article on Fifi. All very positive, I promise. We just want to talk about how she's inheriting your business sense.'

She was clearly going to write the article whether I contributed or not, so I decided I might as well give my side of the story. I ran my comments past my lawyer before sending them to Freya, just to get a second opinion. 'Yes, Fifi does work with various brands specific to children, some of which pay for her services,' I wrote. 'How do I respond to criticism? Each to their own. I don't judge other mothers on how they choose to raise their children, and I don't think it's anyone else's business how I raise my own.'

I thought I made a fair and convincing argument, and that the piece would be positive – but I was thrown to the wolves. I should know, after a decade in my profession, never to read the comments section under an article when it's a personal story about me (and now my daughter). The mummy army had not reacted kindly to me raising an Insta-tot, and had taken to their keyboards in protest:

Posted by: MummaJones

This is so very sad and disturbing. Seriously, what the f*ck is the world coming to? How can we say 'everyone has a right to raise their child as they see fit'? Okay, so child abuse is okay, is it? Everybody should have a choice about whether or not to put their life on social media. Poor Fifi doesn't. She is two years old and doesn't even understand what Instagram is. Money and fame can't buy you happiness – or, in Jasmine's case, class! When you give a child everything – money, attention, fame – there is nothing left to work towards. I think Jasmine will only really understand when she has the next Lindsay Lohan on her hands.

Posted by: Mydaughterskeeper

How does she have an account when she is under 13 years old? It makes a mockery of all the efforts we go to in order to protect children's privacy. When we openly ignore rules we teach our children bad habits. It's no wonder respect is fast diminishing in our society with parenting like yours. It's all very amusing now I'm sure, but this profile will be around forever, and could cause your daughter embarrassment in the future. When you start making money from it you're exploiting your toddler, no matter how innocent your intentions.

Posted by: Stayathomer

Two words: pure narcissism! This sad excuse for a mother needs to take a good, hard look at herself.

I read this stream of bitchy comments while waiting in my office for my bank manager to arrive. I wanted to set up a new savings account for Fifi, who was now a tax-paying sole trader with a steady stream of income. My daughter, the Insta-superstar, was sitting at my boardroom table drawing a picture of a white cat wearing black sunglasses. She had been begging for a kitten, ever since she saw Karl Lagerfeld's cat Choupette. I didn't think the Four Seasons would be that accommodating.

How could people call me a bad mother when in every single photograph of Fifi she was grinning from ear to ear? If her social media career caused her any pain, unhappiness or discomfort I'd shut it down in a second. She genuinely loved it – and it was a great mother–daughter bonding activity.

While I was contemplating my parenting approach, my phone rang. It was Michael. This was a novelty during the working day as he only usually called at 9 pm to say goodnight to Fifi. When I saw his number I kicked my office door closed with my foot, and flicked the phone onto speaker so that Fifi could hear her daddy.

I realised putting Michael on speaker was a bad move when I heard the tone of his voice. 'Jazzy Lou, what the HELL is going on? I've got reporters calling my office asking if I'm exploiting Fifi for CHILD LABOUR!'

Oh, come on, people, I wanted to scream, *are you MAD?* This was now getting ridiculous. Although the publicist in me was pretty impressed that Fifi could get so much attention. Better to be talked about than not . . .

When I didn't answer Michael straight away, he must have taken my silence for a guilty conscience. 'Where are you, Jazzy Lou?' he asked. 'Actually, that's a stupid question. I bet you're at the office, aren't you? Surprise, surprise. Look, stay there. I'm coming to see you and Fifi. We need to talk face to face.'

Within ten minutes my husband was marching through the door of the Queen Bee office, straight past Lulu who was sitting at reception surrounded by two hundred huge blow-up lilos that we were using for a marketing stunt. I was surprised – and slightly annoyed – by Michael's swiftness in getting here. It proved how easily he could make time for us, even at midday on a Wednesday, when he really wanted to.

At the sight of her daddy, Fifi leaped out of her chair and ran to him. It was actually a very sweet moment – father and daughter reunited. By coincidence, they even had on vaguely matching outfits, as I'd dressed Fifi that morning in a Ralph Lauren striped t-shirt and khaki shorts, which were almost identical to Michael's (it must have been a casual day in his office). They looked like the cutest odd couple, standing side by side. Hmm, this probably wasn't an appropriate time to ask for a his-and-hers photo for Instagram, was it?

Instead, I went straight on the defensive. 'Look, Michael, I'm really sorry. I didn't know that it would escalate. The opportunity just arose. Let me explain and you'll agree that I made the right decision, I'm sure.'

I had a whole speech ready to go, but Michael held his hand up to silence me. 'Let's not talk about it in the office, Jasmine,' he replied. 'Now I'm here, I may as well take you two out for lunch. I'm guessing you haven't eaten. Fifi, where would you like to go?'

Of course this meant we ended up at McDonald's. (So much for her mature palate. All a kid ever really wants is a Happy Meal.) As we sat in a booth with sticky plastic seats, I tried to avoid getting grease from the table on the sleeve of my Céline shift dress. Gah, this was dry-clean only. I also tried not to flinch every time Fifi bit into a chicken nugget, deep-fried in god knows what. Was she too young to put on a juice cleanse? Only joking! I actually had a massive craving for an M&M McFlurry. Perhaps I could order one 'for Fifi' and then help her to finish it. Isn't the only good thing about a lovers' tiff the fact that you have an excuse to comfort eat?

The thing you should know about Michael and me is that we have very different parenting styles. He has a specific – and sometimes very old-fashioned – idea of what a family unit should look like. The child is the centre of the universe, the father is the main breadwinner, and the mother dotes on both of them. You may wonder, then, what he was doing with me. I'm not offended if you're thinking that – I asked myself the same question, often.

Michael hid his traditionalism while we were dating – it only really came to light after our honeymoon when we were settling into 'matrimonial bliss'. Now that I had a ring on my finger, it seemed he expected his wife (eugh, even that word makes me squirm) to manage the household, do his washing and press his trousers. Despite the fact that I'd never once cooked him a meal, he still thought it was my responsibility to feed him, and clearly hoped that one day I'd morph into Nigella Lawson . . . or Sophie Dahl after she ditched being skinny to write a cookbook. He expected me to know what was for dinner even before breakfast. Umm, whatever you want from the menu at Beppi's Italian. My culinary skills extend to placing a takeaway order or booking a table for three.

Michael had a hands-off approach to household management, which was fine with me, as long as he didn't expect me to be hands-on either. We both had stressful careers, therefore neither of us should have to cook or clean, but he still thought it was my duty. Hah! I don't even boil a kettle. Why would I when there's a cafe on every corner?

I couldn't really blame Michael for his outdated opinions, as he was only reflecting the way he was brought up. His dad worked in advertising and his mum was a housewife. It was like a scenario straight out of *Mad Men*, with an abundance of whiskey and casual sexism.

While I moved out of my parents' house when I was seventeen, desperate for independence, Michael lived at home until he was twenty-four. What motivation did he really have to flee the nest when he could live rent-free in a six-bedroom house in Watsons Bay, with a mother whose sole purpose in life was picking up after the men in her family?

I understand it is a generational thing because my mother did the same, but then she had a midlife crisis three years ago and almost left my father. 'What do I have to show for my life?' she'd pleaded to him. 'I've spent a lifetime picking up after other people. I need to find myself.' Instead of leaving him, Mum took up a range of new hobbies, including pottery and sky diving. I'd learned from her mistakes and refused to be a doormat for Michael's polished Gucci brogues.

But Michael's mother had never rebelled. In fact, she seemed to think being a mother was the ultimate reward, and that her grown-up son was the ultimate trophy. That's the only example of a family dynamic that Michael's ever had. He wasn't familiar with the idea of a wife and mother who ran her own multimillion-dollar business, a wife and mother who had hustled morning, noon and night for every cent she'd earned and wasn't about to go down quietly.

When Michael had walked into my office that afternoon, I'd been about to grovel for forgiveness. I even considered offering to delete Fifi's account and remove her from The Talent Hive's books, but the drive to the fast-food restaurant had given me time to think. I wasn't going to apologise for my actions. Okay, maybe I should have told Michael what I was doing, but I had tried to call him . . . once.

So, rather than apologise, I tried to appeal to his business brain. 'Michael, don't be angry. It's a smart business opportunity. What mother doesn't spend all day taking photos of her kids? We're just fortunate that for Fifi it can have a profitable component. I'd be a bad parent – and a bad businesswoman – if I didn't make the most of it.'

My better half opened his mouth to say something, then shut it again. 'Oh, for fuck's sake, Jasmine. I'm not angry,' he muttered, looking exhausted. 'I'm just disappointed that I seem to be the last one to know about Fifi's new profession. Do you know how embarrassing it is when a reporter knows more about my daughter's life than I do? We're meant to be a team. I'm meant to be her father.'

His iPhone was lying on the table and I noticed that his screensaver was a photo of the three of us, taken at Disneyland during a holiday to Paris. It had been a pre-honeymoon honeymoon, about six weeks before we got married. We're all wearing Minnie Mouse ears and Fifi is sitting on Michael's shoulder, clutching his hair. I remember I'd freaked out that morning because the theme park didn't have phone reception, but it had been a blessing in disguise. In the photograph I look relaxed and happy. I remember I'd even eaten a cheese-laden burrito for lunch (well, half a burrito, let's not go overboard).

I picked up Michael's phone and smiled at the photograph. 'Oh my god, do you remember how terrified Fifi was of Donald Duck?' I asked. 'I think she was just offended by his hat, to be honest. Oh, Michael, when did we stop having fun? When did we stop laughing like this?'

Do you ever feel so tired that it's just too much effort to be happy? I spent so much of my day with a fake smile plastered on my face that by the time I got home to my husband I was totally out of cheer. The main factor to blame for our breakup (hang on, brain, don't get ahead of yourself) was the nature of the modern world. I can count on one hand my friends' relationships which have stood the test of time. Every week, marriages seemed to be busting up around us, as romance took second place to work commitments, troublesome kids and tax bills.

As I wallowed for a moment in self-pity, Michael reached out and held my hand across the table. I realised it had been weeks (eight, even nine?) since we'd actually had any physical contact. Sensing that her parents were having a moment, Fifi placed both her hands on top of ours, as though we were a sports team about to enter an arena.

Unusually for me, I felt tears prickle my eyes. I do not cry unless it's a life or death situation (such as when a cup of coffee was spilled down my Vera Wang wedding dress ten minutes before I walked down the aisle). Yet I suddenly remembered how nice it was to be part of a family unit; a trio who pulled together, rather than a lone operator.

'Michael,' I said shyly, 'why don't you stay at the Four Seasons with us tonight? I'd really like you to stay over.'

I was already concocting a plan. If I cancelled my morning meeting with the bigwigs at Westfield Shopping Centre, asked Anya to attend the Coles fashion shoot in my place, and convinced Lulu to chaperone Savannah Jagger to the *Cosmo* magazine bloggers breakfast, I'd have some time free. We could have a lie-in . . . until at least 9 am. It was unheard of for me to delegate my responsibilities, but maybe it was time I put my husband's needs first . . . or at least equally. We could order the hotel's signature breakfast in bed (coconut bircher muesli and avocado smashed eggs) and I could finally get around to testing out the spa bath . . .

Then I realised that Michael was looking awkward. 'I'd love to, Jazzy Lou, really I would,' he said, 'but I'm flying out to New York on the red eye this evening. That's why I could take this afternoon off to see you. I'm on my way to the airport. I'll be back in a week or so.'

A week or so? That sounded alarmingly open-ended. And he had the gall to accuse me of not keeping him up to date on my life developments. I might not tell him about every sniff, cough or business deal I made, but I would always tell my husband if I was planning on leaving the country.

'When were you going to tell me?' I responded angrily. 'What if I had to go away on a business trip this week too?

Who would look after Fifi? Do you just expect me to take the brunt of the childcare? Is this why you wanted to stay at the house while we moved out, so you could act like a bachelor? Out of sight, out of mind!'

I knew my voice was getting louder and that if there was one thing Michael hated it was couples who aired their dirty laundry in public. But as my Bees will testify, I tend to shout first and ask questions later. Why do you think a gossip columnist had once nicknamed me the 'perfumed steamroller'?

It may not be a good thing, but Fifi is used to raised voices, and was now once again engrossed in her French fries. She only looked up when Michael screeched his chair back, rising to his feet.

'I'm not going to sit here and argue with you, Jasmine. I was going to tell you – I *did* just tell you. I don't need to ask your permission; I'm not one of your bloody employees. I just wanted to meet up today so we could regroup and check in.'

Regroup? Check in? The problem with having two people in a relationship who are businesspeople is that we both find it hard not to speak in corporate jargon. What about missing me, wanting me? What about sweeping me off my feet, snogging my face off in the middle of a public courtyard? I may have been watching too many rom-coms. But, still, a girl should feel special.

I glued a glare to my face as Michael looked at his watch. 'I'd better go,' he said. 'I'll send you an email when I land to let you know I got there safely.' We had driven to lunch from my office in separate cars, so we didn't even have the drive back to make peace.

He kissed me on the top of the head, then did the same to Fifi, who put on her 'not bothered' game face – and then started crying the moment her daddy was out of sight, naturally.

9

My first thought when I heard rustling in the bushes outside the Queen Bee office that morning was 'wild animal'. Paranoid? Probably! But I had been at work since 5.30 am writing a press release for I'm a Celebrity . . . Get Me Out of Here! (the reality TV show had just signed up Foxy as their next series' totty) and I had snakes and spiders on the brain.

It wasn't only tiredness making my brain foggy. After my argument with Michael yesterday, when Fifi had fallen asleep in my double bed I'd had a little 'party for one' in my hotel room. It wasn't my fault . . . really. I blame freaking room service.

The downstairs bar was having a themed night to celebrate the wedding of the hotel's owner. According to the menu card left propped on my pillow, they were serving two special cocktails: a Soulmate Mohito and a Bitter Single Sour. I chose the latter, which said a lot about my frame of mind. I think the porter assumed I had company, because he brought it up in a cocktail mixer which contained the equivalent of four glasses of liquid.

And it tasted far too nice for its own good. I suspect the concoction was ninety-nine percent watermelon liqueur, because my tongue was now green and my head felt like it was the size of a bowling ball. I hate feeling out of control so I only get drunk maybe once or twice a year, and my body just isn't used to it. I felt like I'd flown long-haul . . . in economy. Eugh! If only I hadn't sworn off the Nurofen after my stomach-pumping incident some years ago (I had had just a little bit of a dependency once and my therapist said that even a taste of the sugary pill coating could spark a relapse).

Thank goodness, Alice, my salvation, had arrived at 5 am on the dot to take care of Fifi. Apparently I'd texted her the night before asking if she could come early because it was an 'emiargenceee' (she'd worked out that my drunken slurring meant 'emergency'). According to my iPhone I had also taken approximately 5600 selfies (okay, I may be exaggerating) of myself wrapped in a fur coat Shelley left behind when she visited last week. I vaguely remember pretending that I was Liza Minnelli. Thank fuck I didn't post any pics.

'Umm, are you okay, Jasmine?' asked Alice when she let herself into my hotel room. 'Are you sick? No offence, but you look just a little bit . . . peaky.'

From Alice's expression I could tell it was bad. Should I paint a black cross on my door and be done with it? I'd tried my best to gloss over my pasty complexion, but I felt too clammy to put on foundation and my hands shook too much to commandeer a mascara wand.

Usually, my go-to pep-me-up dress is a black number by Givenchy, but while impressive, it's also skin tight and unforgiving. Just thinking about squeezing the contents of my stomach into that dress made me want to vomit. Instead, I'd opted for my version of comfort dressing. No, not trackie pants. Come on, people, I'm a fashion publicist with a hangover, not some university student. I was wearing a navy stretchy shift dress by Bassike which covered a multitude of sins (it had actually been part of my maternity wardrobe) and flat Charlotte Olympia sandals with straps that tied up my calves. I didn't even have the energy to pick out accessories, so my only jewellery pieces were my engagement and wedding rings. I briefly thought about taking those off too, after my spat with Michael the afternoon before; but no, that was childish. Plus, I live in a hotel room – it was probably best not to leave $600k worth of jewellery lying around.

'I'm fine, Ally,' I said in a hushed voice. 'Don't worry about me. Just burning the candle at both ends as usual.'

She didn't look convinced but was too professional to push it. I gave Fifi a squeeze, as she lay on my bed watching *Dora the Explorer*, and then prepared to face the outside world. Luckily, there were few people about because it was only 5.20 am. As

I drove down Oxford Street, there was really just me and the ravers falling out of the nightclubs. They looked how I felt . . .

I was in my office by 5.30 am, after parking haphazardly in the underground car park. It's unusual these days that I'm ever in Queen Bee headquarters alone, because I've groomed my staff to work the same crazy hours as I do. But I love the rare occasions when I have the giant open-plan office to myself, especially before the sun comes up. Sometimes I still can't believe that I built this empire by myself.

I left the lights off and crisscrossed through the racks of clothing to my office, running my hand across Alex Perry, Oscar de la Renta and Jil Sander. Ah, my old fashion friends, you never let me down.

When I booted up my computer, I saw that my husband hadn't remembered to email me, even though he'd landed in New York when I was only halfway through my first cocktail, according to his flight status on the Qantas website. As my screensaver I had a photograph of Michael, Fifi and me taken last Christmas (all three of us were making #thelipsthelips at the camera), but that morning it was proving distracting, so I switched it to Belle Single's police mug shot. The reality TV star had just been caught drink driving (for the seventh time). This made me feel slightly better. I may be a lush, but at least I'm law-abiding. I settled down to write my press release.

As the Bees began to filter into the office at around 7 am, they also assumed from my dowdy appearance that I must be ill. 'Jazz, you look terrible. Is it Fashion Week flu? Have you been overdoing it?'

I was offered everything from Berocca to echinacea, and a mystery red pill that Anya claimed would either kill or cure me. Tempting! I told my staff I just had a migraine, which everyone seemed to buy – except Lulu. My personal assistant knows me better than my own mother, and at 7.30 am she popped her head around my office door and handed me a cup of nuclear-strong coffee.

She gave me a stern look. 'Jazz, I've made you an appointment in half an hour at the Alkaline spa in Potts Point,' she declared. 'Ten minutes in their detox sauna and you'll sweat out that . . . migraine. It's a miracle cure, I promise you.'

It's not often I leave the office to have a beauty treatment in the middle of the day, but this was an emergency. I had a meeting with a health blogger that afternoon and needed to not look like shit (or smell like melon liqueur).

'Thank you, thank you, thank you,' I whispered to Lulu as I grabbed my bag and she accompanied me to the exit. 'If anyone asks, I'm at the gynaecologist. Actually, don't say that. They'll think I'm up the duff. Just say I'm in a meeting.'

I blinked as the glare of the morning sun hit me, thankful for my new Céline sunnies with the extra-dark tint. And that's when I heard the rustling in the bushes and nearly jumped out of my skin. Oh fuck, what was that? Could my Birkin work as a shield against a python?

But, hang on a minute, this wasn't a snake. It was an even slimier lurker . . . fucking paparazzi. I almost had a heart attack when he leaped out of the lavender bushes and pointed his camera lens in my direction. What was he doing skulking outside our office? Had he confused me for a celebrity? But no, this time I was the story.

By mid-afternoon, photos of me were splashed across the *Daily Mail* website. I'd made the infamous 'sidebar of shame' – you know, the section where they show stars without makeup or exercising in unflattering sports gear.

After more than a decade working as a publicist, this wasn't the first time I'd been stalked by paparazzi, but they were usually after the celebrity I was chaperoning, not me. However, the *Daily Mail* had a new love affair with all things Australian. It had been announced a fortnight before that the newspaper was launching an Aussie version of their website. Suddenly our isolated island and our small-fry celebrities were on their radar: Delta Goodrem, Ricki-Lee and even Jesinta Campbell were starring in *Daily Mail* articles. And now even my personal life was newsworthy:

> Australian PR queen Jasmine Lewis looked tired but chic as she left her office in inner-city Sydney this morning, wearing her hair tied up and minimal makeup.

In case you didn't know, this is tabloid talk for 'looking like shit'. It's just like when you tell a girlfriend who has put on weight that she looks 'healthy' or 'voluptuous'.

I still didn't think that me exiting my own office was a headline-grabbing story, but the real gossip was still to come. The article continued:

The afternoon before, Jasmine was spotted having lunch with her husband Michael Lloyd, with eyewitnesses saying the conversation looked 'tense' and 'heated'. The socialite and her investment banker husband embarked on a whirlwind romance in 2010 and married in Sydney's wedding of the year in 2012.

Great, this was just what I needed. Michael was going to kill me. One of the reasons his relationship with Belle Single fell apart (aside from her neediness, greediness and sneakiness) was the that fact he hated being part of the media circus. He overlooked the odd article written about us in the Australian newspapers, because he knew I needed a local profile, but he wouldn't be impressed if our family made international headlines – especially when the story was so close to the bone.

And who were these 'witnesses'? Was I being followed? Come on, Jazzy Lou, I thought, don't let your ego get away with you – there are far more important people to spy on. It must just be bad luck. Maybe a journalist happened to have a craving for a Big Mac and overheard our ruckus. Stranger things have happened.

I forwarded a link to the article to Michael, with the subject line: 'Better you see this from me . . .' I didn't want to give him an excuse to think I was hiding anything. His reply was short and to the point: 'Next time kick the pap in the nuts.' Well, at least his anger wasn't being directed at me . . .

However, the media intrusion didn't end there. I wasn't the only member of my family to make headlines that week. On Sunday morning, as I flicked through the latest issue of gossip mag *Now*, circling in red biro any mention of my clients, I came face to face with a photograph of my father strolling out of a restaurant in Los Angeles . . . and he wasn't alone. The headline read: 'Does struggling socialite Tessa Blow have a new sugar daddy?'

My father is just an average Joe – a successful businessman but a nobody in the media world. However, his holiday companion lives her entire life shamelessly in the spotlight. Thanks for telling me that you have a new girlfriend, Dad. A postcard might have been a better way to break it to me. But no, I had to read about it in the paper like the rest of the country:

Is this the new Brynne and Geoffrey Edelsten? *Now* has acquired exclusive photographs of Sydney socialite Tessa Blow—the former wife of billionaire hotelier Maximus Blow—on a romantic holiday with businessman Ned Lewis. He is the father of Sydney PR powerhouse Jasmine Lewis, and is over two decades older than his 28-year-old girlfriend. The buxom blonde is currently in the midst of a messy divorce from her husband, who owns six hotels and three casinos, in Australia, Dubai and Singapore. In a high-profile court case, she is fighting the terms of her pre-nup, which states she has no entitlement to her ex's fortune.

Before marrying up, Blow worked as a personal trainer but quit to pursue a career in music, releasing her first single, 'La-La-Love', in the early noughties, which sold just 1200 copies, according to a spy I have in her record label.

Questions will be asked about who paid for the lavish holiday as the couple were caught leaving The Bazaar restaurant, famous for its smoking cocktails and jaw-dropping price tag. They were also seen booking into the Beverly Hills Hotel.

Who needs money when you have new love?

When I got to the end of the article, I took my red biro and drew a moustache on Tessa Blow's photo. Then I drew a speech bubble coming out of her mouth which read, 'I am a gold-digger.' I added another speech bubble coming from my father: 'I am a gullible idiot.'

He couldn't have picked a more inappropriate love match. It was well known on the circuit that Tessa had only married Max for his money and was devastated when he'd ordered her out of their mansion after discovering her in a clinch with her personal trainer (okay, this was all rumour, but there's no smoke without fire). Suddenly many pieces of the puzzle fell into place – why five months ago my father had suddenly upped and left my mother with no explanation.

They must have met at the party I threw at The Marquee to celebrate the launch of The Talent Hive. I don't even know how Tessa had slipped onto the guest list, but she certainly made an entrance, arriving in a nearly nude dress that made Rihanna look like a nun. I'd noticed Dad talking to Tessa by the DJ booth but hadn't thought anything of it. If only I'd intervened, I could have played reverse wingman and stopped their union. I suddenly knew how Dad must have felt when, aged sixteen, I'd brought home a twenty-eight-year-old 'slam poet' called Phoenix.

At least there was little chance of my mum spotting the article. She was currently in San Tropez. I'd bought her a one-way ticket after my dad's 'I'm leaving' revelation so she could recover at a health spa in luxury. It didn't have wi-fi (bad for your chakras apparently) so she would be none the wiser about my dad's dalliance.

Lucky her! I couldn't get the picture out of my head. And I'm sorry to be selfish, but didn't Dad realise that this could seriously damage my reputation? I really didn't want to be associated with a D-lister like Tessa and give the press any more reason to delve into our family affairs.

I grabbed my iPhone and punched in a message: 'Dad, when were you going to tell me about Tessa? Really? *disapproving face*'

Then I felt bad and sent him another: 'P.S. What happened to your beer belly? You're looking great.' Credit where credit was due. I just hoped he hadn't lost weight through sexercise. Eugh, vomit.

What was wrong with the men in my life at the moment? What was wrong with all the people around me in general? My two-year-old daughter actually seemed to be the only one with a sensible head on her shoulders.

10

After the stress of the past few weeks (new business venture, relationship speed bumps, Dad's floozy), I decided I needed an emotional outlet outside of the office – a way to release some tension and take my mind off my problems. I haven't had a real hobby for years – who does when they're an adult? My career is my leisure activity, and attending VIP parties is my pastime. When I do have a rare night to myself, I really don't have any way to fill it. The highlight of last week was eating a Cornetto in bed while watching *Game of Thrones*.

However, I was starting to think an extracurricular activity could be good for me – especially if it was something involving exercise. Since the night I'd binged on Bitter Single Sours, I had been on a bit of a downward spiral when it came to my health and wellness. Again, I blamed room service. It was far too easy to access any drink you chose at any hour. And it wasn't just booze; I'd also been mainlining coffee. So much for my vow to cut back on caffeine — I'd lasted less than twenty-four hours on green tea before I fell off the wagon and ordered a double espresso.

All these extra toxins, combined with the stress of launching a new venture and worrying about my relationship, were wreaking havoc on my nerves and my skin, which had broken out in zits. Although another side-effect was that the stress was supercharging my metabolism so my skinny jeans were feeling looser — there's always a silver lining. Yet I knew I couldn't continue firing on all cylinders as I'd soon hit burnout. The last time that happened I'd ended up in hospital, which was inconvenient enough when I was single, but now I had Fifi to think about.

It was time for a body reboot, and I knew just the girl to advise me. The Talent Hive had just signed its latest client — a health blogger called Florence Lilac, who writes under the pseudonym Flossie Love (if I ever have another daughter I'm so stealing that name).

If you want to feel like a fat, vice-ridden lush just stand within ten feet of Flossie, who is a glowing vision of vitality, dressed in floaty white cotton, fuelled by cacao smoothies and kale chips. The health guru even carries a miniature esky everywhere she goes so she is never tempted to 'indulge' in food she hasn't prepared herself. During our first meeting, we shared a picnic on my boardroom table, consisting of gluten-free sprouted loaf with activated almond butter and chia seeds (which I spent the entire meeting picking out of my teeth – how very professional).

'You have to tell me, Flossie,' I begged during our next meeting, 'how do you stay so cool, calm and collected? I can't imagine you ever being frazzled.'

Unlike many bloggers, who think posting a photo a day is a full-time job, Flossie works like a demon. As well as her website, she also designs her own active-wear range, and was about to launch an all-natural fake tan (the secret ingredients was spirulina, which stopped you turning orange).

'Shall I tell you my secret?' Flossie beckoned me to lean in closer. Oooh, yes please. Was she about to tell me about some magic pill that would boost my energy and my concentration, while also calming my nerves and boosting my libido? Wouldn't that be the answer to every woman's prayers?

I'd once ordered a supposed 'superwoman pill' from the internet, after watching a news report about it on *A Current Affair*. It was a drug usually prescribed for kids with ADHD, but stressed-out career women were abusing it to make themselves more focused. I think the news report was meant to be a warning, but I saw it as an advertisement. Unfortunately, Michael opened my mail and banned me from taking it (probably a good move, considering my history with over-the-counter medication).

I should have known that Flossie's secret strategy would be a whole lot more . . . wholesome. As I leaned forward, she whispered in my ear the one word I'd been dreading. It began with 'Y' and rhymed with 'toga'. Groan! She was one of them.

I should have guessed: when she arrived for our meeting, she was dressed in purple Lululemon tights and a vest top that read 'Spiritual Gangster'. Also, she greeted me with 'Namaste'.

It turned out that not only was she a dedicated yogi, but she was the type who wanted to recruit everyone else to join the revolution. 'I really think you should try a yoga class, Jasmine,' she enthused. 'I spent six months at an ashram in India, studying under Guru Gama Yama Yala, and it changed my life.' As if to prove a point, she jumped out of her seat and demonstrated a 'warrior two' pose in the centre of my office (to me it looked like a lunge with some added angry arms thrown in).

'I used to be just like you, Jasmine,' she went on. 'Tired, stressed out, overworked, grumpy. I thought it was normal to feel anxious all the time. But now I practise yoga every day and I'm a different person. Really, you don't know how good your body and mind can feel until you've tried it. It's cosmic!'

I wasn't about to admit this to Flossie, but I had once tried a yoga class, when I was on honeymoon in the Seychelles. The luxury resort ran classes every morning. The experience didn't end well; in fact, I was evicted ten minutes into the class and banned from the studio. The teacher claimed my mobile phone was disturbing the other students, but I refused to put it on silent. I would be far from zen if I missed a call from the head of Versace in Italy. We were on the verge of a business deal . . . I'd thought yogis were meant to be accepting, but I've sensed less judgement at an X Factor audition. As I was being escorted from the class, the woman on the mat next to me tutted loudly, as if I had committed a cardinal sin.

I'd thought that incident had put me off downward dogging forever, but maybe it was time to give yoga another whirl. Maybe it would not only (hopefully) make me more tranquil but also give me some muscles. Fifi was getting bigger and my arms were straining to carry her (and our matching handbags). I'd taken a slight exercise hiatus of late. The Four Seasons has a heated swimming pool, and when I moved in I'd vowed to add fifty lengths a day to my schedule. Sadly, the one time I'd visited the pool area I'd got distracted by the jacuzzi and sauna, and hadn't even got my hair wet.

The hotel also has a fitness centre, with high-tech machines that look like they belong on the NASA space station. Reception even provides gym wear to all the guests, handing you a t-shirt, shorts and socks. Although this was very generous, it was not a plus point for me. I do not like arriving at an event in the same outfit as someone else, whether it's a VIP party or an exercise session.

I used to work out with a colossal personal trainer called Andy 'Tank' Jones (you might recognise him from the last series of The Bachelor). The muscle machine had helped me tone up for my wedding, but had then selfishly gone and got himself a lead role in the musical Tap Dogs. The last thing I heard he was in the West End and dating the leading lady from Legally Blonde.

I had searched for a replacement but it was difficult – both to find a spare hour in the day to work out and also to find a trainer who was compatible with me. A lot of the personal trainers in the health-conscious Eastern Suburbs of Sydney are just too . . . good looking. Really, they look like Hollywood movie stars (only with better tans and surf skills). I know you're thinking, 'What's she complaining about?', but I am not one of those women who look good when they exercise. I turn red, my hair frizzes, sometimes I come out in a sweat rash. The last thing I want is some Adonis standing over me as I fall apart. I want a trainer who is good looking enough to be motivational, but not so gorgeous as to be intimidating.

'Will yoga give me a body like yours?' I asked Flossie. 'I don't mean to sound creepy but you have one hot bod! Although I'm sure you're told that all the time.'

Flossie laughed and accepted the compliment, which I admired her for. When a girl is unquestionably stunning, why waste time with false modesty?

'Oh, it will definitely help you tone up,' she assured me. 'Although it's not really about looking good, Jasmine. The best thing about yoga is it enhances your inner beauty. As my guru says, yoga isn't about self-improvement, it's about self-acceptance.'

I was gagging to reply, 'Screw inner beauty! I just want glutes of steel,' but I knew that wouldn't be very ohm of me. Instead, I asked Flossie to recommend a good yoga school in my area – preferably a class where I wouldn't have to chant or change my name to 'Lotus' to be accepted.

In this city, yoga studios are opening on every street corner and charging premium rates for a pick-me-up. I didn't know where to begin: Bikram, Vinyasa, Hatha, Kundalini? I also wanted somewhere 'shiny'. A lot of yoga studios, in Bondi in particular, advertise themselves as 'authentic'. This really means 'shabby'. If I'm going to lie on a rubber mat, it's gotta be in a high-class establishment. Luckily, Flossie understood my requirements and recommended the newest yoga school in the trendy shopping district of Surry Hills, owned by an ex-fashion model turned yoga teacher called Sasia Abraham.

I knew a bit about the Flexi-Time studio already, because Queen Bee had organised the launch party when it opened the previous summer. It was all oakwood floors, mirrored walls and spa-like changing rooms with complimentary Jo Malone toiletries (I'm sure the Dalai Lama would approve).

After my conversation with Flossie, I checked their timetable online and noticed that they had a mother-and-toddler class called Yoga Hop ('Think the Wiggles meets yoga. A workout for mothers and their offspring'). Usually I'm not big on mum-and-daughter workshops. For some reason, other mothers don't seem to like me. However, this did sound interesting, and less intimidating than a standard yoga class. Hopefully it would mean nobody would take it too seriously, and the kids would be the centre of attention so nobody would notice my lack of coordination.

It would also provide great fodder for Fifi's Instagram page. In my head I was already wording the caption:

A girl's got to work on her core. I want the best abs in my playgroup. If you think this figure comes easily, think again. It's hectic keeping healthy. #treepost #zen #fitspiration

On top of this, it would be a great excuse to go shopping. I'd heard rumours that funky fitness label The Upside might be bringing out a junior range, and I could just imagine Fifi and me in matching crop tops and yoga pants.

I was really starting to warm to this yoga malarkey, but I still felt like I needed a bit of moral support. Hmm, who had time on their hands and would be willing to risk ridicule for me? I could order Lulu or one of the other Bees to come with me, but there was a better option – Shelley!

Now, I have never seen my best friend do anything that even vaguely resembles exercise. I did see Shelley run once – but it was across the fragrance section of David Jones to grab the last bottle of limited-edition Balmain perfume. Surely it was about time she elevated her heart rate again.

'Shells, I've decided we need to take up yoga,' I texted my friend. 'Next Wednesday. 7 am. Lock it in your diary.' As Shelley doesn't work, you can always rely on her to reply to a message before a 'read receipt' arrives. When I hadn't received a response from her an hour later, I knew her silence meant no – and so I pulled out my secret weapon.

A few weeks ago, I'd read on Women's Wear Daily that Gucci were bringing out a special-edition yoga bag. Made in the signature Gucci print, it was designed to hold your mat and a yoga block (whatever that was). And it was 'only' $2300.

I texted Shelley a link to the bag on Net-A-Porter, with the message: 'The answer to eternal happiness . . .'

Within moments my phone beeped with a message. 'You manipulative cow. I'M IN!!!' It was as easy as tempting a soccer player into a strip club.

A week later, I found myself in a room full of lycra-clad mothers and children in leotards, sitting cross-legged and humming in unison. Toto, we're not in Kansas anymore . . .

Beside me sat Shelley, dressed in an all-in-one playsuit by Stella McCartney, which she'd ordered from StyleRunner on an overnight delivery. And in front of her sat her surrogate child for the day, a two-year-old girl with blonde pigtails, wearing an identical outfit.

The yoga school had given Shelley permission to attend the mother–daughter class solo, but she had insisted on finding a miniature plus-one to bring with her. 'Really, Jazzy Lou,' she cried, 'when have you known me not to have the right accessories? If it says bring a child then I am damn well going to bring one. Is there a place that hires out toddlers?'

In the end, she'd 'borrowed' a little girl from a friend with twins who was happy to loan out her spare. Before the class, Shelley took her fake daughter Poppy for a manicure, and her tiny fingernails were now painted with yin and yang symbols. It may sound cheesy but I was kind of jealous. I'd only colour-coordinated Fifi's coral nails to her headband. How slack of me!

According to our teacher, Sasia, the 'bee breath technique' we were practising was meant to balance the two sides of our brains and help us to both stay alert and relax. If I'm honest, it was just making my nose tickle, and Fifi must have felt the same, because she had two fingers stuck up her nostrils.

I was also distracted by Sasia's breasts, which seemed to have grown three cup sizes since the last time I saw her, and were defying gravity in a tiny strappy crop top. Wasn't it against a yoga teacher's code of ethics to have plastic surgery? I wondered how a boob job fitted into all this talk of self-love and inner peace. But, hey, who am I to judge?

As we bent, stretched and flexed along with Sasia, I have to admit it felt good to be moving. My lifestyle choices are not kind to my skeletal system. I spend my days either crunched up at a desk or sprinting around in five-inch heels, lugging a Birkin that weighs as much as my toddler. As Sasia guided the mums into a bridge, and the children crawled underneath us, my spine creaked and cracked (in a good way).

Next up, we lay on our backs and kicked our legs like upturned turtles. *Do not fart*, I willed my body, *or at least not until someone else does first!* Fifi was in her element — as was Shelley. My best friend had a huge smile on her face and was looking at Poppy adoringly as the little girl wiggled and giggled.

I had always thought Shelley hated children, as whenever a mutual friend of ours gave birth, Shelley always sent the biggest bouquet of flowers but said she was too busy to visit in person. The only child I'd ever seen my best friend interact with was Fifi, and I'd sometimes suspected that she might be a little jealous of her. Naturally, our friendship had shifted slightly when I became a mother, and Shelley couldn't understand why I could no longer just fly to New York for a shopping weekend with no notice.

Yet as I watched Shelley help her fake daughter try a roly-poly, she looked perfectly natural playing the part of a parent. Did Shelley have a maternal streak that I didn't know about?

It's funny how, even though Shelley and I share everything, we'd always skirted around any mention of her lack of boyfriends or whether she was broody. That said, I also never uttered the b-word before having Fifi. My biological clock hadn't even started to tick when Michael and I had our happy accident.

When the class was over and we were sipping dandelion lattes in the cafe beneath the yoga studio (where harem pants and prayer beads seemed to be the dress code), I gently raised the subject: 'How fun was today, Shells? I can feel my butt tightening already. You know, fake motherhood suits you. You're one yummy pretend mummy . . .'

For a second Shelley looked embarrassed, then she quickly recovered. She took a bite of her vegan bliss ball, and said with her mouth full, 'Maybe I can find a fake man to inseminate me. Ooh, maybe you and I can live in a man-less share house. A child only needs two parents, right? Well, one and one mum makes two. We wouldn't need any guys at all.'

I think she was joking, but I can never be quite sure with Shelley. And where would Michael fit into this scenario? Where indeed . . .

11

As we'd exited the yoga studio after my debut mummy-and-toddler class, Sasia had chirruped, 'Same time, same mat tomorrow, yogis!', but there was no chance I'd be back in the morning for a do-over. I had a breakfast meeting at The Grounds of Alexandria cafe to discuss them hosting a launch party for the Doncha Wanna Be Us fashion line (yep, the girls were adding another string to blogging bows).

I was glad I'd left Fifi with her nanny before dropping by the cafe. There are some things a two-year-old doesn't need to witness, and that includes her grandfather pashing his new girlfriend in public like a couple of teenagers. I really didn't know what had got into my dad, who was usually a stickler for social etiquette.

I had just strolled into The Grounds, automatically scanning the eatery for any people of importance (it's a force of habit in my profession), when I spotted a silhouette on the coach in the corner on the other side of the room. Actually I spotted a familiar bald patch, as I could only see the back of his head because my father was too busy playing tonsil-tennis.

'Are you kidding me?' I muttered, my instinct telling me to get the hell out of there. But it was too late. My favourite barista Joey — a South American exchange student who works there part time — had spotted me and cried out, 'Jazzy Lou! Where's that beautiful daughter of yours?'

Despite the fact my dad was a good twenty metres away from us, Joey's enthusiastic greeting could be heard across the room and both he and Tessa looked up like a couple of meerkats.

'Jasmine!' he called, waving his arm in a beckoning gesture. 'What a surprise to see you here.'

Was it a surprise, Dad? Really? I've been coming to this cafe constantly ever since it opened, as my Instagram page would testify from the #coffeeselfies I often posted from there. Why did I feel like it wasn't a coincidence he was here? Why did I feel like I was being hijacked?

In retrospect, I should have just made my excuses and not gone over. But, by this stage, Joey was standing awkwardly behind me with a coffee. 'Jasmine, where shall I leave your drink? Over here with your . . . friends?' Oh, fuck it. I'd give them a few minutes. The person I was meeting was running late anyway.

As I approached the table, the new addition to my family greeted me with two air kisses (that was fine) and then enveloped me in a bear hug (not so fine). Tessa then made a joke that was much too much, much too soon: 'Jazzy Lou, it's lovely to see you. Isn't this a turn-up for the books, me dating your father? You can call me step-mummy. Hahaha!'

I raised my eyebrows and forced out a chuckle that sounded more like I was being strangled. I didn't voice my thoughts aloud as it simply wasn't worth the confrontation, but I was thinking that for you to be my step-mother my dad would need to act like a father and he had turned his back on those responsibilities when he turned his back on my mother. Bite your tongue, Jasmine. Bite your tongue.

'Isn't the coffee here just life-changing,' exclaimed Tessa, waving her lipstick smeared cup. 'We haven't been getting much sleep lately, if you know what I mean.'

Oh my gawd! Don't wink and nudge me. You're talking about the man who changed my diapers. I really, really didn't need to know about their slumber parties.

I knew Tessa hadn't officially moved in with my father yet, because I'd read a news story in *The Sun* only yesterday about how she was renting a five-bedroom mansion in Double Bay at a cost of $4000 per week. 'TESSA BLOW HAS NOT LOST HER TASTE FOR LUXURY!' screamed the headline:

Despite an imminent divorce case which may leave her with nothing, Sydney socialite Tessa Blow doesn't seem to be counting the pennies. The singer, who left the home she shared with husband Maximus Blow after their marriage ended last year, has now upsized to an even larger property in Double Bay, which she is renting.

Despite her troubles, the 28-year-old's lavish lifestyle does not appear to be suffering. Last week she was spotted strolling through her new neighbourhood with one of her collection of Hermès Birkin bags worth thousands, and stepping out of her Ferrari 458.

Ah, the Ferrari. This was another sore point for me. It was Tessa's pride and joy, but I'd heard on the grapevine weeks ago that because it was in Max's name, she'd been forced to leave it behind when she fled their matrimonial home. Max had then decided to sell it, not wanting any reminder of his former love. Well, guess who the buyer was? My father. How romantic, buying your girlfriend's car off the husband she'd cheated on. It now sat in my father's driveway, still bearing the personalised number plate 'T3SS'.

I knew I shouldn't judge her too harshly before I saw how their relationship panned out. And I had to admit that my dad did look well. I shudder to use the phrase 'he was glowing', but it did seem appropriate. His eyes were shining and he'd definitely lost weight since I'd last seen him, which had been the week he announced to my mother he was leaving her (deep breath, hold your tongue!).

'So how have you been, Jasmine?' asked Dad, draping his arm across Tessa's shoulders, his fingers playing with the strap of her sport's vest. I wish they could just stop touching each other for one moment.

'I'm very well. Thank you for asking.' My response had as much emotion as an automated telephone-banking clerk. I wasn't going to give him anything.

It also looked as if *somebody* (one guess who!) had been influencing Dad's dress sense. For years I'd been trying to get him to dress more imaginatively, but he just bulk-bought polo shirts from Target; refused to wear labels, claiming they were a waste of money. Now, my papa looked like a slave to fashion, dressed in a Tom Ford sweater I'd recently been eyeing up for Michael on Mr Porter. He was even wearing a pair of suede slippers I recognised as Jimmy Choo. And was that a necklace peeking out of his collar? OMG! My dad was actually accessorising! I suspected he and Tessa had been on a shopping spree. On *his* credit card, I betcha!

For a few minutes (that felt like hours) our trio made small talk. It helped that Tessa and I moved in the same social circles and could exchange industry gossip – did you hear that so-and-so is back with her ex? And did know that Channel Six is sacking so-and-so for a younger hostess?

Tessa also raised the subject of Fifi's Instagram feed, claiming that she was her 'biggest fan'. She even pulled out her iPhone (the latest diamond-encrusted version, worth $5600) to show my dad the photos I'd taken at our yoga class.

Then my dad cleared his throat. I knew that sound . . . Uh-oh. What was coming?

When I was little my father would take me along to his office on school holidays, where I'd hide under the table while he did business deals. I'm sure that's where my entrepreneurial streak came from. When I was ten, I'd noticed that my dad has a 'tell' when he's about to say something a colleague or client might not be happy about. And now I was on the other end of that awkward cough, which meant I probably wouldn't like the next sentence to come out of his mouth.

'Jasmine. It's actually a lucky coincidence we ran into you. I wanted to talk to you about something,' he started. 'In fact, we both wanted to talk to you.'

I had a sick feeling in my stomach, which wasn't from Joey's perfect beverage. My instinct told me that the reason my dad had clearly laid in wait for me at the coffee house wasn't going to please me. Until this point I'd been standing awkwardly next to them, but he gestured for me to take a seat and, like an obedient child, I did. Why is it that, at any age, our parents seem to hold some power over us?

'As you know, Tessa is currently . . . tying up some loose ends with her marriage. As part of the divorce proceedings, her husband's lawyers are calculating how much she owes and how much she owns in assets – real estate, possessions.'

I really should have put a stop to the conversation there, but I let my father continue as I had a feeling he'd practised this speech and was about to reach the grand finale.

'In the interests of protecting Tessa's assets,' he continued, 'she needs to do a little bit of careful . . . reallocation. We thought you might be able to assist by storing a few personal items she'd rather the court didn't find out about.'

At this point, Tessa put her hand on my father's arm and butted in. 'Let's cut to the chase, Jasmine,' she said. 'We're all grown-ups here and we're all businesspeople. Locked in a safe in my flat I have $800,000 worth of diamonds that my husband bought me. I'm not about to give them up without a fight.'

I had heard all about Tessa's infamous diamond addiction. In fact, in her music video she sang naked wearing only a diamond choker. That chick was classy. According to whispers, she'd had enquiries from the Victoria & Albert Museum in London, who were interested in buying the vast collection, because a lot of the items were vintage. Which meant the divorce lawyers would surely already know about it too.

'So, what exactly do you want me to do?' I asked, directing my question at my father. Was he really asking what I thought he was?

'We wondered if you could . . . look after the diamonds for Tessa . . . for both of us,' he replied, looking embarrassed. 'It wouldn't be for long – probably a few months at the most. It's just until the courts reach a decision and all this mucky business is over and done with.'

I couldn't believe he was asking his own daughter to commit a crime, and for the sake of a woman he'd known for a matter of months. Where was the loyalty? Where was the concern for my safety and my reputation? If it came out

I'd helped her swindle the courts, Queen Bee could also go down in flames.

'Umm, Dad, can I speak to you alone?' I asked politely. 'I don't mean to sound rude, Tessa, but there are only certain trusted people I talk business with, and I'd like to talk to my dad separately.'

She raised her eyebrows but didn't protest. 'Sure, whatever. I need to return a phone call outside anyway,' she said. 'Think about it carefully, Jasmine. I know you don't owe me anything, but my welfare also affects your father now. If I'm happy then he's happy, remember that.'

As she exited the coffee shop, I noticed the red sole of her Christian Louboutin shoes still had the sales stickers on the bottom of them (she'd probably try and take them back after she wore them). Then I turned my attention back to my father.

'Dad, how could you hijack me like that?' I said, trying to keep my voice low, as I really didn't want the whole cafe to know our business. 'It's bad enough you'd ask me to do something like that in the first place, but you should have asked me privately. It is not cool, calling a "family meeting" with the three of us.'

I felt like freaking Cinderella, faced with an evil stepmother. I bet Tessa would steal the crystal slipper from my foot if given half a second – and my dad would probably let her.

'Don't exaggerate, Jasmine,' he replied. 'And don't pretend you wouldn't do something similar if you were in Tessa's situation. I can't imagine you'd be happy to give up the lavish lifestyle you're so used to. Imagine if Michael ever walked out on you – god forbid. Would you give away the things you've worked so hard for, or do everything in your power to keep them?'

The difference is, dear Daddy, I would never get myself into that situation in the first place. Okay, once upon a time I might have been guilty of leading a million-dollar lifestyle on a $30,000 salary (and several credit cards), but I now only spent as much as I earned, and I never relied on Michael for a handout.

'That's totally irrelevant,' I huffed at my father. 'And I don't appreciate you trying to guilt-trip me into committing a crime. In case it's escaped your attention, I have a two-year-old daughter, your granddaughter. What about *her* welfare?'

It was time for me to leave. My blood was starting to boil and I needed to get out of there before I said something I would regret. I'd also just seen my breakfast meeting companion walk through the door. I had Talent Hive business to deal with and I wasn't going to let Dad's soap opera get in the way of that.

When I'd witnessed Tessa and my father snogging on the sofa, I had for a moment considered the notion that I might just be jealous. Was I really envious that Dad was dating like a teenager while my own relationship was fizzling? But no, my gut reaction was right. This woman was a gold-digger and a con artist, and she and my dad were welcome to each other. I'd made my decision.

'You can tell Tessa it is a resounding, unequivocal, never going to happen NO,' I told them. 'I don't ever want to talk about this again. What you decide to do is your business, but

I am not being dragged down with you. Oh, and here's one piece of advice – if you want to fool people into thinking you're poor, you might not want to be photographed at a five-star hotel. Come on! Have some common sense!'

I didn't even give my father a chance to reply, as I spun on my heels and slapped on a happy smile to face my next meeting. Through the cafe's big, open doorways I caught sight of Tessa, with her phone pressed against her ear, leaning against a fence in the courtyard. The problem was that the gate lead to the home of the cafe's pet . . . a pig.

Quickly I pulled out my phone and snapped a shot. Tessa jowling into the phone, unaware the cafe's pet porker had stuck his head between the fence posts and was currently taste-testing the trail of her dress. It was the perfect double portrait, although I wasn't mean enough to post in on social media. But it was good to have in my arsenal (and it certainly made me laugh!) #twinnies.

12

Forget fathers, the only man a woman can rely on is her interior designer. Put that slogan on a greeting card and I'd buy it. As the men in my family continued to disappoint me, at least I could rely on Jackson to boost my mood. I woke up every morning to at least three texts from my creative soulmate, with an update in the form of a photo essay of whichever part of my house he was currently transforming.

At the moment, it was the bathroom. The theme was 'Midsummer Night's Dream'; the bathtub was the centrepiece, according to Jackson, and was made of solid walnut wood. Yes, a bath made out of wood. If you think it must look like a boat then you're spot on the money. Jackson had modelled it on Michael's yacht, the *Adventuress*, which he parks (docks, moors, whatever the word is) in Sydney Harbour. He only takes it out once a year, on New Year's Eve, to get a good view of the fireworks.

Unlike my husband, my interior designer didn't think my 'quirks' were annoying — in fact, Jackson seemed to thrive on the challenge. Aside from my wardrobe, my bathroom is where my OCD really kicks in. I need everything to be impeccably planned, organised and structured. Clean your teeth, put your brush back in the concealed cupboard, place the toothpaste tube back in the silver toothpaste squeezer (yes, such a contraption exists, google it). Is your towel hung up on the heated rail, folded into a perfect rectangle so you can see the FRETTE logo on the bottom right-hand corner? It better be, buddy! Okay, I admit I have issues, but Jackson didn't mock them, he worked around them.

He'd even built a display case into the bathroom wall to store my toiletries in chronological order of expiration date. He'd also made all the bathroom cupboards sensor-operated so they didn't need handles. This impressed me on two levels: no ugly handles ruining the lines, plus it was far more hygienic. I'd just have to teach Fifi that not all cupboards can be opened by waving your hands over them. That could be really inconvenient when she started preschool.

All in all, Jackson was proving to be a godsend, even if the interior project was taking far longer and costing far more than I'd initially intended. I was glad that something in my life was going smoothly — even if it was just the wallpaper.

The Saturday after the argument with my father, I decided to visit my house to see how the work was progressing. I needed something to cheer me up, as the row with Dad was causing me sleepless nights (and a girl needs her beauty sleep).

Since our fraught family meeting, neither of us had tried to contact the other. My dad seemed to think that I'd done something wrong and he was sulking. Pleeease! He was lucky I hadn't leaked Tessa's plan to the press – or dobbed her in to her husband's divorce lawyer.

I had, however, dobbed him in to my mother, his ex-wife. I didn't mean to. But when Mum had called from St Tropez, she had asked how my father was keeping and I didn't want to lie. So I filled her in on exactly how he was doing – and who he was doing it with.

My mum wasn't too impressed, especially as it turned out that her second cousin, a plastic surgeon, had given Tessa a little nip-and-tuck a year earlier and was still waiting for her to pay the bill. Who wasn't she trying to fleece out of money?

I know I shouldn't have told Mum, because it would surely stir up trouble, but whatevs! I wanted my team to be bigger than Dad's was. He could expect a strongly worded postcard to arrive in the mail any day now, postmarked Europe. 'Wish you were here . . . wish you weren't dating a gold-digger.'

Before heading to the house, Fifi and I swung past Westfield for some retail therapy. First we hit up Sass & Bide, then Armani, followed by a visit to the Nike superstore to stock up on yoga gear. I was really getting into this fitness malarkey. Well, I hadn't yet attended another yoga class, but

I had stocked up on gear. It turned out that sports kit has come a long way since gym knickers, and I'd swapped my Net-A-Porter addiction for StyleRunner.com and The Upside.

After a few hours and a lot of credit card scanning, we called it a day. Call me superficial, but I did feel better. I snapped a mega-cute photo of Fifi laden down with heavy carrier bags, clutching her arms with a pained expression on her face. I posted it on Instagram with the comment:

My mum says I'm suffering from 'shopper's elbow'. Need to build up my muscles. Shopping bags are the new dumbbells. #retailworkout

That post got 819 likes – the numbers were going up every day.

By the time Fifi and I made our way back to the car, we were both shattered. When we pulled into our driveway, Fifi was fast asleep in her Gucci car seat, so I decided to leave her there with the door open so she had plenty of air and I could listen out for her while I did a quick tour of the house to see how it was developing. I also didn't want to risk her running into any wet paint. Fifi had chosen her own outfit that morning and had erred on the side of impractical. I'm not sure why she even owned a pink furry dress and an orange feather boa – or why she thought they went together – but she insisted.

I left my little muppet snoring in the car seat and let myself into my old–new home. It even looked different from the outside, as Jackson had changed the front door to a high-tech version which opened with a buzzer key ring. The first thing I noticed when I entered the house was the cream and leather panelling which now covered every single wall . . . in every single room. Call me over the top, but once you bite the bullet you may as well go the whole hog.

Jackson had left a note for me on the kitchen table: 'Remember, it's not finished! You shouldn't open an oven door before a soufflé has risen.' Oh, these crazy queens. He had tried to put me off coming at all, but I wasn't going to be barred from my own home. Anyway, he was just being a perfectionist (which was why I'd hired him in the first place), because the house looked spectacular, even though it was semi-covered in dustsheets.

The sleek cream-coloured furniture came from Cavit & Co, and I'd asked on of my Talent Hive creatives, a fashion illustrator called Felicia Penfold, to create a one-off piece of art to go over the fireplace.

Jackson had done an ah-mazing job, so I texted him: 'I am HERE. I am astonished. You are the ultimate remodelista!!'

My interior maestro is a Grindr addict so is always glued to his mobile. I knew he'd reply instantly, and he did: 'You like it? PHEW! Who am I kidding, I knew you'd love it. How splendiferous is the leather coating on the fridge? It's the same one as Tom Cruise has! Although that husband of yours didn't seem so impressed when I showed him yesterday. Philistine!'

I was about to write back telling him not to listen to Michael — what did he know about interiors? — but then

Jackson's text sunk in . . . Michael. Yesterday. He was meant to be in New York. He couldn't be home. Why wouldn't he tell me?

That's when I heard a noise from upstairs. A thump and a shuffle, as if someone had got out of bed and was walking across the bedroom.

'Umm, hello?' I called, automatically reaching for my Birkin and iPad, which were on the kitchen table. If I had to run from an intruder, I was taking life's essentials with me.

I turned to see a silhouette of a man in the kitchen doorway. That man was my husband, dressed in grey linen pyjamas, looking decidedly jetlagged. Although it was two o'clock in the afternoon, he'd clearly just woken up, which made me think he must have only flown in yesterday.

'Michael, what the hell are you doing here?' I asked, as he rubbed sleep from his eyes. I should have been happy to see him, but I felt infuriated . . . and hurt. I didn't know how long he'd been home, but if it was long enough to manage a freaking conversation with my interior designer, why hadn't he come over to see me?

'Hey, Jazzy Lou,' he said, crossing the room to kiss me. 'This is a nice surprise. Is my little princess with you? I was going to come over and see you this evening. Oh, come on, don't glare at me like that, Jazzy Lou. I really didn't think it was worth calling you earlier as I know you work most Saturdays these days.'

Despite the pyjamas, which are not an item of clothing I think any grown man should own, my husband was looking dishevelled and gorgeous. It felt like so long since we had slept in the same bed that I'd forgotten how adorable he looked just after waking. I didn't want to hold a grudge now that we were finally reunited. As Fifi was asleep, maybe we could christen the newly decorated bedroom.

I gave in, put my arms around Michael's waist and nestled my mouth into his neck in a way that I know always gets him excited. But after a moment, Michael pushed me away. 'I'm dying for a coffee,' he moaned, glancing at the state-of-the-art espresso machine that Jackson had installed. 'I think that thing makes coffee, but I can't for the life of me work out how to use it. Why don't we own a fucking kettle?'

I told myself not to be offended by the rebuff, or his grumpiness. He was jetlagged, he was tired, he was clearly not in the mood – a long-haul flight isn't exactly a libido booster.

'I can see if Lulu's close by and can pick up a coffee order,' I said, pulling out my iPhone. The best thing about having employees who are addicted to social media is that you can easily track their movements. Ah, see, Lulu had updated her personal Facebook page two minutes earlier, and it showed her location as 'Redfern, Sydney'. Even I couldn't ask her to come all this way to grab me a coffee on a Saturday.

Then I remembered a new app I'd downloaded called Coffee Runner, which promises to deliver a coffee order to any location in Sydney within ten minutes. Time to road-test it. Sure enough, exactly eight minutes and fourteen seconds after I logged our request, a guy on a motorbike screamed up outside our house and handed over two non-spill cups.

I don't know how he did it, driving through Sydney's winding streets, but the chocolate dusting on the milk foam was still in the perfect shape of a love heart. That was well worth the $12-per-cup of coffee price tag, in my opinion.

As soon as Michael took a sip, a mask seemed to fall from his face and he instantly looked more alert (yes, we're addicts, but it's not like it's heroin). He then uttered the words that no wife wants to hear. 'Jasmine, we need to talk.' My stomach filled with butterflies – although that could have been the caffeine kicking in.

I took a seat at one of our new kitchen bar stools (polished chrome, very ergonomic, very uncomfortable), and Michael sat down opposite me at the countertop. My husband is a very smart businessman, very eloquent, used to public speaking. I knew that if he was going to deliver bad news, it would be clear and succinct. Just how I prefer it.

'Jasmine, I might be working away for a while,' he said, looking stern. 'It could be for up to five years.' What was he talking about? Why would he 'need' to go away? As I sat in stunned silence, trying to digest the news, Michael filled in the details. The reason behind his trip to New York had been a job interview with Chad Turner. The Chad Turner whose motivational CDs he was so fond of.

'I didn't want to tell you before in case I jinxed it,' Michael said excitedly. 'He wants to launch a new financial coaching program – how an average Joe can become a millionaire. He wants me to oversee the whole thing: plan the twelve-step program, run seminars from Madison Square Garden. Can you imagine! And you should see their offices. They have sleep pods where you can take a power nap.'

I frowned. When did my husband become impressed with corporate gimmicks like that? He'd once turned down a job with Google because they had a pool table in the middle of the office. He'd told me this on our first date, and it was one of the reasons I fell for him. And what about me? What about Fifi? And why the five-year time limit?

'They want to test whether I'm committed,' he explained. 'Apparently, the last guy who had the job quit after a year, at a crucial time for the company. I can leave whenever I want, in theory, it's not like they're locking me up, but my contract states that if I leave before the five-year mark I have to reimburse them financially. But I'm not going to want to, Jazz. Why would I want to leave my dream job?'

In his enthusiasm, there seemed to be one factor that Michael was forgetting. 'Umm, how about your daughter?' I asked, my voice going up an octave. 'You're talking about living in another country from us for the next FIVE FREAKING YEARS. Fifi will be seven years old before she can wake up in the same home as her daddy. Or are you asking us to move to New York with you?'

He looked embarrassed, and I realised he hadn't even thought about that option. Not that I would have said yes, but it would have been nice to be asked along on his emigration adventure. Seriously.

'Oh, come on, Jazz. You would never leave Sydney. This is your world. These are your people,' he replied, sounding just a little disparaging. 'I was going to ask you to come. You could run Queen Bee remotely, but I know you're such a control freak. Could you really leave your business, your baby, in someone else's hands?'

Annoyingly, he was right. The Talent Hive was at a crucial point, just starting to get some momentum. I'm not just the boss, I'm the brand. How could I walk away? At the end of the day, it's my bottom line and my reputation. That's why I still dictate every fucking email that goes out of Queen Bee. Okay, that's a bit of an exaggeration, but I do proofread them all. If you speak to any journalist, they will tell you I am the girl who answers their calls, whether it's midnight or 6 am, Monday to Sunday. How could I micro-manage my company from another country twelve hours behind us?

Plus, while I love New York for Christmas shopping, I didn't think I wanted to live there. I had once thought about it, at the very start of my career (too many *Friends* box sets), but the PR scene in NYC wasn't really in keeping with my style. Too much pale skin, too many Cosmopolitans . . .

I rounded on Michael. 'I can't believe you're talking as if this is no big deal. This is a HUGE deal. I know things haven't exactly been smooth between us recently, but it's going to be a hell of a lot harder if you're not even here for us to kiss and make up.'

I don't know why I was bothering to argue, because he seemed to have already made up his mind. This wasn't a conversation for us to weigh up the options; it was a declaration. He'd probably already booked his flight and organised his freaking going-away party.

As if he'd read my mind, Michael said, 'Of course, Jasmine, if you ask me to stay I will. You and Fifi are my priority. They've given me five weeks to make my decision. Chad is going to climb Everest and then Mount Kilimanjaro, and I don't need to tell him until he gets back. We can talk some more about whether it's the right decision.'

I knew it wasn't the right decision – how could it be? But he was certainly determined to convince me. Forget this new role: the way he was spinning this job offer, my husband should think about a career as a politician.

'Jazzy Lou, I really think this could be good for us,' he argued. 'We both have such busy lives and so many commitments that we barely see each other anyway. We can make the most of the time we do have together. The apartment they've offered me overlooks Barneys. You'll love it. It'll be like a mini honeymoon every time you visit.'

I noticed he kept talking about me visiting him but not about him visiting me. Our 'mini honeymoons' were clearly going to be carved out of my schedule, rather than cutting into his time. And what about the carbon-footprint-thingy of jetting back and forth to the US? I'm not usually environmentally minded (after all, my recent publicity stunts have revolved around cars and disposable coffee cups), but I was searching for any reason why this move shouldn't happen.

I don't think Michael even heard me. 'It's only a nineteen-hour flight, even less if you go by private jet,' he said. 'I'm happy to pay. I want to make this as painless for Fifi and you as possible. This doesn't need to be a bad thing, Jazz. Lots of couples live apart. They call them the "live a-partners". I read an article about it in the *New York Times*. I'll dig it out for you. I know how you love being part of a new trend . . .'

Who was he kidding? We both knew that if he took the job it would probably spell the end for us. I never dreamed I'd be the type of wife to say this – god, I was turning into such a cliché – but it really was the job or me. The unspoken ultimatum hung in the air between us.

So this was my new reality. My husband might be leaving me. Fuck, I was going to be a single mother. Oh sure, I'd still be married, but only in theory. If a husband says 'I love you' in New York, and no one is around to hear, does it still count?

I had five weeks to convince him not to go. But did I really want to beg?

13

A good friend of mine, a fashion publicist who works in Los Angeles, once said that PRs are the best matchmakers. If you want to find a man, place your love life in a publicist's hands. Oh, don't get me wrong, we're utterly useless when it comes to maintaining a relationship ourselves. The traits that make a girl a good PR make us terrible girlfriends. We talk too much, we judge too harshly, and we just can't help checking our iPhones during dinner (and even during sex). It's all part of the job requirements. Yet when it comes to other people's love lives, we're modern-day cupids (if Cupid swapped his arrow for an iPhone with the private number of every eligible bachelor in the city programmed in).

The thing about publicists is we know everybody – and I mean everybody. We also work in an industry where the woman-to-man ratio is five to one. It might sound like a disadvantage when you're man-hunting to exist in an environment where females vastly outnumber the opposite sex. However, there's one thing you should remember: most of the women who work in fashion are a guy's idea of hell – high-maintenance and fussy, self-involved and insecure.

Most of the rare straight guys who work in fashion are desperately seeking a normal girl. Oh, they may want a model as a conquest, but not as a long-term companion. This is where the fashion publicist can play cupid, and set the guy up with her friends who don't work in the business. We'll also vet (translation: stalk) every man via social media before setting him up with any of our friends. Our credibility is at stake!

Plus, as an added bonus, we can provide the perfect venue for your first date. Forget meeting at a restaurant. How about soccer tickets, a party on a floating island or an overnight stay in a luxury tent at Taronga Zoo? We have the contacts and the sway to make it possible. Impressed? He will be too.

We also know exactly how to sell a product (or, in this case, person) in one short, snappy slogan. This comes in handy when you're communicating in text-talk. If you ever want to win over a guy (or win an argument) via text, first send any message to a publicist friend. We are ruthless editors and will make sure the message cuts to the chase and is neither too needy nor too nonchalant.

By second nature, publicists are game-players. Some people see this as a negative trait, but it's all part of a publicist's tool kit. (Note to self: I should really start up an online dating site.) We can spot a fake a mile off, and fake it ourselves when we need to. It's a set of skills that comes in handy in our profession, as well as in the romantic arena.

That's why when a certain Australian cricketer started 'liking' all of Queen Bee's photos on Instagram – even the boring ones I had to post to please clients – I knew straight away he had an ulterior motive. This wasn't just politeness, he was flirting. Gen-Y style.

Hayden Smith had recently split up from his actress girlfriend after a five-year long-distance relationship that captivated the media's attention. His ex was an actress who lived in Hollywood and had left her husband to be with him. Now there were rumours of affairs on both their parts, and mud was being slung by each camp.

If Smithy's history was anything to go by, the serial dater wouldn't be single for long. He had hooked up with his former girlfriend after they started flirting on Twitter, so he was no stranger to finding love (or at least lust) on social media.

Maybe I was reading too much into it. Smithy might just have a genuine interest in the photos he 'liked'. Maybe he was a secret connoisseur of Crème de la Mer, coconut water and scented candles (three of the clients I'd chosen to keep in the cull).

But then it started to get ridiculous, and the 'likes' turned into comments. What did he do, spend all day checking Instagram just waiting for me to update our page? Or was he Insta-stalking a bunch of women?

Although Smithy, like myself, was a long-running fixture of the Sydney social scene, we'd only met once, at a charity gala held at the Sydney Football Stadium. His then girlfriend had been wearing a dress covered in tassels, and as I brushed past her the metal studs of my clutch bag got caught on one of them. I'd quickly untangled myself and we hadn't even stopped to make small talk. The extent of our interaction was: 'Oops, so sorry. Haha. Have a good evening.'

But now it seemed we were best friends, bosom buddies. He posted two-word comments at first. 'Nice wheels' underneath a photo of me posing next to my Range Rover, and 'Yum yum' next to a picture of me sitting at my desk at 9 pm tucking into a tub of frozen yoghurt (another client, and I only had a spoonful). But then his emoticons amped up a notch: a love heart, a little yellow face blowing kisses. This was definitely Insta-flirting. I was glad his comments were buried among hundreds of others so nobody else would notice, especially when he started commenting on my outfits.

Recently, Rosa had come up with the bright idea of posting a photo of my outfits to Instagram every day. We knew from our bloggers that style diaries got a lot of attention. It had been a savvy suggestion, as *Bizarre* magazine instantly picked up on it and asked if they could print the photos in their September issue – with the heading 'A day in the wardrobe of a fashion publicist'. I didn't let it go to my head – it was cheap and easy content for them as we weren't making them pay for the photos. And yet it was all good publicity, and gave me a reason to get even more creative with my ensembles.

In fact, I was secretly using the daily posts as a way to stick one finger up at Michael. I know, very mature of me. Since my husband had made his announcement about the job offer, all I'd wanted to do was throw a tantrum. The problem was I was meant to be convincing him to stay (there were now only four weeks left until he needed to make his decision). If I ranted and raved too much he would be on the next plane to the Big Apple.

So on the rare occasions we were in the same vicinity, I played nice. Michael still insisted on sleeping at the house to oversee the reno, but he did come to visit the Four Seasons every weekend. Instead of causing an argument, I rebelled in the only other way I knew how – through the medium of fashion.

I started choosing every outfit that I knew Michael really hated. Just call me the new Man Repeller. My arsenal of fuck-you clothing included harem pants, boyfriend jeans, jumpsuits and anything with shoulder pads. These were all items of clothing Michael didn't understand and wished I didn't own (he'd told me this once when he was drunk).

The ultimate 'up yours' was a spotted Céline shift dress that I adored but which Michael said made me look the size of a house. I think he was being sarcastic because I had asked him for the tenth time if my bum looked big in it. Either way, we'd had an almighty row and I'd never worn the dress since (would you after that comment?). However, in the aftermath of the New York conversation, I dug it out of my wardrobe and gave it an outing. I was going to wear what I wanted, and if he didn't like it he could find a freaking New York girl who lived and died in skinny jeans and an oversized sweater.

I made sure the photograph of the Céline was taken at the most flattering angle, and added a black and white filter (always a good option to up the class factor). I was pretty pleased with the result, if I do say so myself. I even texted it to Michael to remind him what he'd be missing. His response wasn't exactly emphatic: 'Very nice.' Not even a kiss. Don't go overboard, bud.

Luckily I had the Insta-sphere for validation. Before long, there were thirty-six comments under the photograph (not quite in Fifi's league but still a good result), complimenting the frock and asking where I'd got it. I hashtagged a reply: '#celine #lastseason #soldout #sorrypeeps'.

Then I noticed a familiar face in my list of commentators. Apparently Smithy was a fashion expert as well as a fast bowler. 'What an outfit!' he wrote. 'Dressed to kill. That should be illegal.'

I have to admit that after my husband's lack of enthusiasm, I was happy to accept the compliment, but I wasn't going to reply. Although whatever I said would be very innocent, Instagram is far too public a platform to be exchanging comments with a known womaniser. It seems Smithy had the same thought, as he decided to swap mediums and sent me a direct message on Twitter:

Jasmine, I need you. Well, I need your services. I'm looking for a fashion stylist. I've just dumped mine. Can you do me over?

Ah, how very interesting. Everyone knew that Smithy's ex-girlfriend used to dress him. And he knew that I knew. This man spoke in euphemisms and was also, I suspected, looking for an excuse to see me. Or maybe I was imagining it. Lack of attention from a significant other can do odd things to a woman. Last week I'd overheard Anya and Lulu complaining about their foundering love lives. 'Is it a bad sign that I spend so much time with my iPhone that I've changed my screensaver to a picture of a hot guy, just to feel less lonely?' said Anya. 'I've even given him a name, and I talk to him sometimes.' I really must tell my employees not to make admissions like this in public.

Now I summoned Anya into my office. No, I wasn't about to bring up the 'man phone', I was going to use her as my gatekeeper. 'Anya, I just got a message from Hayden Smith,' I explained. 'He's looking for a fashion stylist and wants a recommendation. I thought Stella Scarborough would be a good match,' I said, naming the hottest Aussie stylist of the moment. 'As long as he doesn't hit on her . . .' I was only half joking. It wouldn't be the first time a male celebrity had tried to seduce a fashion stylist in a changing room. You would think they could come up with a more modern pick-up line than the old inside-leg-measurement trick. Seems not.

'It's probably worth going through Smithy's agent rather than directly to him,' I went on. 'Send him Stella's rate card, but tell him the first appointment is complimentary. A gift from Queen Bee.'

This was the kind of passive-aggressive flirting I'd mastered when I was a single twenty-something. In my younger days of dating, Smithy was exactly the type of inappropriate suitor I'd have gone for. Like most young PR girls, I just wanted to be part of a power couple, and my wish list, in order of importance, was 'wealth, looks and social standing'. Nowadays I wasn't that easily impressed, or that naive. I would soon be able to tell if Smithy genuinely needed a stylist, or if it was all part of an elaborate courtship ritual.

I didn't have to wait long. Anya soon poked her head around my office door. 'I've just spoken to Hayden,' she said. 'I'm sorry, Jazz, I know you told me not to go to him directly, but I left a message on his manager's voicemail and Hayden was the one who called me back.' She continued, reading a message that she'd scribbled on a notepad: 'He says that while it's very generous of Queen Bee to offer a free styling appointment, he wondered if someone more senior and experienced could help him.' She looked up from her notepad and laughed. 'He wants to know if you'll take him shopping, Jazz. Shall I tell him he's dreaming . . . politely, of course? I mean, really, what is he thinking?'

I bet I could guess exactly what Smithy was thinking. Oh, he'd know I was married, but this cricketer had the morals of a *Big Brother* contestant. 'Do you have his number there?' I asked Anya. 'I'll take it from here, don't worry. These bloody sports stars, huh! They think they can click their fingers and the world will come running.'

I should have sent Smithy an email and set him straight. From both a professional and a personal standpoint it would have been the right thing to do. So why did I fold up the note with his phone number on it and slot the piece of paper into the coin holder of my Hermès wallet, in between a photograph of Fifi and a bundle of cab charges? (I don't keep small change in my purse. I've been known to pay for a forty-cent chocolate bar with plastic.)

Maybe I could take Smithy shopping just once. He was an iconic Australian celebrity and had serious media power (even if it was often for the wrong reasons). I don't like to miss out on a networking opportunity. Also, it wasn't that absurd a suggestion. I do know my fashion. And I could see it as an act of charity. I had to get him out of those terrible V-neck t-shirts his ex-girlfriend had insisted on dressing him in.

I did once harbour a dream of being a fashion stylist, or even a designer (until I realised that I can't replace a button on a shirt, let alone design and sew an entire collection). Even now I can't help feeling a glimmer of envy when I'm backstage at Fashion Week watching the creative process unfold. There's something so romantic about seeing a dress go from sketchpad to reality, like a cartoon character coming to life. Well, now it looked like I might be able to live out my fantasy . . . through my daughter. Oh my gawd! I never thought I'd become one of those mothers.

My two-year-old was about to add fashion designer to her repertoire. Not only was she the best-dressed baby and sassiest selfie-taker, she was also going to be the 'miniature milliner'. As part of my daughter's brand evolution, I had decided she would bring out a range of headwear. It was official – I had just registered the company name, 'Fifi's Fascinators'. Snappy, huh? You can't go wrong with a bit of alliteration in a marketing slogan.

The next step of Fifi's career had happened organically. Since her Instagram account took off, people had been going crazy for the decorated headbands my daughter loves to wear. She has a collection of artistic headwear to rival Lady Gaga's; some of the headbands have bows as big as her head, while others have flowers and pom-poms.

Her current favourite was a woolly beanie with a black veil that hung over her face ('If Rihanna can do it, so can I,' I wrote on Instagram). She also loved the hairband that had a giant plastic lobster attached to the top, and another with an enormous cherry the size of her head. They were very Anna Dello Russo.

A lot of Fifi's headwear was one of a kind – gifts from designer friends such as Mary and Christopher Kane, who made them especially for my munchkin. Others I ordered on the internet from Japanese websites usually favoured by Harajuku girls.

Every time I put one of the headbands in Fifi's hair, Michael would say, 'Don't make her wear that ridiculous thing.' But my daughter loved them, and so did her Insta-followers.

In launching the range, I was only giving her fans what they wanted. And it wasn't just a range for children – I constantly had adults asking where and how they could buy Fifi's headbands. That's why I'd ordered the designs in kiddie and grown-up sizes.

I'd found a factory in China that could manufacture Fifi's Fascinators on the cheap for me. The first batch was already being shipped and would arrive in time for the launch of Fifi's website in May.

We were planning a launch party at the QT Hotel in Sydney, and I was currently trying to convince Philip Treacy to fly in from London to host it (we'd met at the Melbourne Cup and hit it off after I ordered a Guinness and blackberry).

I'd even had business cards printed with the Fifi's Fascinators logo, a cartoon of a little girl with a bow in her hair. I'd given Fifi a batch of the business cards to keep in her clutch bag, so she could give them out to her little friends at playgroup (hopefully they'd hand-deliver them to their mothers, who would be our first customers).

The first design meeting for Fifi's Fascinators had been a hilarious and surreal experience. How many meetings are chaired by a two-year-old? I wasn't just putting Fifi's name on the product – I wanted my daughter to be involved in the entire creative process, designing everything from the bows themselves to the packaging, which was equally important (just ask Tiffany). I'd asked Anya to sit in and also invited Shelley, as well as Tara from Doncha Wanna Be Us, as she was a fierce fashion critic.

I was getting the sense that Shelley might be jealous of my burgeoning friendship with Tara. For one, she referred to the blogger as 'the stick insect'. Then, when I'd invited her to an event to celebrate a Doncha Wanna Be Us collaboration with David Jones, Shelley said she was too busy to come. My best friend never misses a social opportunity; I've known her to attend three weddings in one day. I hoped that inviting both of my closest girlfriends to Queen Bee HQ together would help them to bond. I've never been the type to crave a gaggle of girlfriends, but as I got older I had begun to appreciate the value of having genuine female friends, and not just frenemies (there's a lot of faux fellowship in PR and you never know who might stab you in the back).

Tara arrived first to our business meeting, which didn't surprise me as Shelley is notoriously terrible at early rising (our meeting was at 9 am – to her that's the middle of the night). I had to laugh when Tara bustled into my office. 'What are you wearing?' I cried. 'I LOVE it, but where on earth did you get it?'

Tara touched the top of her head, where she wore a huge bow à la Fifi. Except this wasn't any old bow – the fabric was printed with a montage of images from Fifi's Instagram page. There was my little girl feeding the ducks, window-shopping at Chanel, and of course #thelipsthelips.

'Well, I thought this momentous occasion deserved some-thing a little special,' laughed Tara, giving a twirl. 'I have a friend who's a print maker and she made it for me.'

At this point, Fifi, who had been 'helping' Lulu sort through post at reception (translation: playing with bubble wrap), sprinted into the office, then skidded to a halt in her new Minnetonka moccasin shoes, which I'd teamed with Ralph Lauren jeans and a Cotton On smock top.

'Look, Fifi. Can you see what Tara has on her head?' The best thing about the bow was that it wasn't just a novelty item. Somehow Tara managed to make it look cool, teamed with her usual signature cut-off denim shorts and a loose white vest top.

She crouched down to be eye-to-eye with my daughter. 'Guess what, Fifi? I have a surprise for you too!' Her Mulberry tote bag lay next to her and from it she pulled a cream box the size of an orange. As Fifi looked on in wonderment, Tara cracked it open to reveal an identical bow to the one she wore – in a miniature size for the miniature head of my offspring. Seriously, this blogger was a doll!

Fifi and I oohed and ahhed in unison, and then I heard a cough behind me. Shelley was standing in the doorway, wearing a very flattering Dion Lee jersey dress . . . and a frown.

'Shells!' I spun around and hugged her, holding her for a second longer than normal, as I had a feeling she needed reassurance. 'You look gorgeous. Is that a new dress? I'm going to have to get one. Do you mind if we're matchy-matchy?'

Tara, who was busy securing Fifi's new bow in her hair, looked up. 'That's Dion, right? I was going to buy it, but I think all the small sizes sold out fast. Jazzy, you might have trouble finding one.'

I flinched and Shelley's frown deepened. I could see her brain ticking over. *Is she calling me chubby?* It was time to change the subject – pronto!

'I'm *sooo* glad you could all make it,' I cried over-enthusiastically. 'There's no one whose opinion I value more than you guys. Shall we get down to it?'

The five of us sat down with a bundle of sources of inspiration, from glossy magazines and old millinery catalogues to books on the history of fashion. We ripped out pages and pages of ideas and fashioned them into a mood board. Then I gave Fifi a marker pen and let her loose on the mood board, drawing hearts and circles around her favourites.

'I think you should keep the first run as simple as possible,' said Tara. 'Just while we road-test the product.' We decided to initially stick with bows but offer a range of five colours and three different sizes (not everyone wants a bow on their head the size of a dinner plate).

I thought Fifi would soon get bored, but she seemed transfixed by all the colours and patterns. If she hadn't wanted to be involved, I wouldn't have made her. I wasn't going to force her, but it seemed she had inherited her mother's work ethic. Her cheeks were flushed and she giggled excitedly as she tossed around the sketchbook pages

And boy did she have a strong opinion. She was not into the brown at all. 'Yucky, yucky. No, Mummy,' she cried when I showed her the sample. Her favourite was the white bow that looked like it was covered in paint splatters, inspired by a Jackson Pollock painting. I might have to get her a matching dress made too. And maybe shoes. Too much? Hmm.

I was proud of my daughter for sitting still through the entire ninety-minute meeting, especially when she'd had a late night the day before because I'd taken her to the MET Bar, where the bouncer kindly overlooked the fact that she was underage . . . by over a decade.

'Good girl, Fifi,' I told her. 'See how satisfying it is putting in a hard day's work. Now you can watch *Dora the Explorer* safe in the knowledge that you've really earned your down time. Isn't it satisfying knowing that while your friends were having nap time, you've created something special?'

The boardroom bonding also seemed to have served its purpose with Shelley and Tara, who had connected over a mutual dislike of the word 'pleather' and a mutual amusement when Fifi had raided Tara's handbag and smeared her new YSL lipstick across her mouth. Soon they were laughing like old friends.

Usually, after the first meeting with a new client, we'd celebrate the milestone with a glass of champagne or a sneaky midday whiskey, depending on the gender of those involved. I can honestly say I've never before celebrated the birth of a brand with glasses of chocolate milk and Oreo cookies. But then it's not every day you start a fashion empire with a two-year-old. And I had a feeling this was only the beginning.

14

If there's one personality trait I just can't stand in my staff it's a superiority complex. Girls who think they're above certain tasks and, worse, that they're above each other. Nobody is invincible in the PR world, and in the Queen Bee offices we're all on the same level. Well, I'm the top dog, obviously, but beneath me it's a land of equality. And, remember, you're only as good as your last press release.

The problem is that the PR industry seems to either attract or create girls with great big egos. We then teach them how to command a room and be the centre of attention. It's a dangerous skill to instil in a twenty-something-year-old.

These girls arrive on their first day a little shy and apprehensive – and then the transformation starts to occur. I can spot it happening a mile off. Suddenly they're too important to restock the fridge with water, or lug a pile of garment bags up onto the stage after the courier decides he can't be bothered making the fifth trip back from the car. Suddenly, instead of idolising me, you can see in their eyes they've started to resent me. Sadly, I suspect they think they're better than me, and that I should be eternally grateful to have them working for me.

When this personality shift occurs, it's the beginning of the end for our working relationship. Inevitably, things will come to a head in one way or another. I know my staff call me 'the terminator' behind my back because I sack more employees than on a season of *The Apprentice*. However, all my hirings and firings are for very good reasons. I don't actually enjoy showing a staff member the door – especially when I thought they were one of the good guys.

When I hired Rosa I really thought she'd be in it for the long haul; she seemed so down to earth and grateful, especially when I gave her the Queen Bee blog to manage. Maybe it was my fault for promoting my social media guru too quickly. She was now Anya's right-hand woman in The Talent Hive and I'd given her some of our top creatives to manage, including a trio of fashion illustrators we'd just signed up.

But it seemed my faith was misplaced. Oh, Rosa's work continued to be flawless (the publicity stunt where she projected the illustrators' work onto the Sydney Opera House was a stroke of genius). It was her attitude that started to grate on me. 'I really need a new Apple Mac laptop, Jazzy Lou. How can you expect me to work on a model that is six months old?' and 'Do I really have to teach the other girls how to upload content to the blog, Jasmine? I mean, can't they just buy *Blogging for Dummies* and learn that way? I have better things to do with my time.'

On a number of occasions I had to ask Rosa to watch her tone. In the Queen Bee office we're not overly formal. When a staff member is good to me, I genuinely think of them as family, and I often sign off emails to Lulu and Anya with I *love you xox*. But that didn't mean Rosa could speak to me like a stroppy teenager. You're twenty-seven years old, so save your angst for your own time.

As I watched Rosa morph from sweetness to sourpuss, I discreetly started looking for her replacement. I didn't go as far as advertising the position, but did ask my trusted friends in the industry if they knew anyone who might be interested.

When it comes to hiring and firing, I 'make like a monkey'. You know the metaphor – I prefer to let go of one branch only when I have another right in front of me to grab onto. In an ideal world, I won't sack a Bee until I have another girl ready to step into her shoes straight away. It might sound harsh, but in a business as busy as mine, we couldn't afford to be a soldier down.

Fortunately, I had already found a possible replacement for Rosa when she stalked into my office and committed career suicide.

It was Thursday morning, which is the absolute worst time in the PR world to cause a scene, because Thursday is the night most of our press parties are held. The office was utter bedlam: I had Bees blowing up giant helium balloons in the shape of handbags, another group was stuffing goody bags with makeup, and Anya was struggling with a ski simulator machine that was going to an event to launch Nike's new ski goggles. I was praying the snow machine wouldn't go off accidentally. And then Rosa stomped into my office and demanded a word.

'Can it wait?' I asked. 'This really isn't a good time. I have producers from Channel Twelve arriving in ten minutes.' The TV station wanted to discuss filming a reality show in the Queen Bee offices. I'd told them no on more than one occasion (who did they think I was, Belle Single?) but they kept upping the ideas – and the money.

'Soz, Jazz, but it really can't wait another moment,' said Rosa. 'I need to talk to you before I fly out to London tomorrow.'

Maybe I'm far too generous for my own good but, despite Rosa's recent attitude change, I'd still given her a special mission. She was flying to the UK the next day to accompany Savannah Jagger from Dare to Wear to a photo shoot at Glastonbury. The fashion blogger had been hired by the Australian high street clothing brand Stitched to do a festival-themed photo shoot.

In spite of Savannah's reputation for being difficult to handle, all of the Bees had been desperate to take on the assignment. I'd overheard them one morning in the kitchen, animatedly guessing who I might pick to go. 'It's Glastonbury, man! Can you imagine how awesome that'll be? Apparently

Jay-Z and Beyoncé are going to do a duet this year. AND there's going to be a performance from an Amy Winehouse hologram. Epic!'

On top of the thrill of the five-day festival, I'd also decided to extend the trip to a week and send the Bee in question to meet a few select British magazine editors. Many of our fashion bloggers have a global reach, which means they need global media coverage. All in all, it was a trip of a lifetime for a Bee, and one that would seriously boost her CV.

When I'd told Rosa that she'd won the golden ticket, she was delighted. Although the first thing she exclaimed was, 'That's ah-mazzzing. I'm so excited I get to see my boyfriend!'

I know long-distance relationships take their toll, but I would have preferred her first thought to be business over pleasure. Still, I genuinely thought she was the best Bee for the job. There was a clause in Savannah's contract with Stitched that stated she had to post photos of her trip on social media to 'cause a buzz' about their latest collection. This was Rosa's area of expertise. I knew (I thought!) she could be trusted, but here she was, less than twenty-four hours before her flight to Blighty, with what seemed to be an emergency.

'Fine, fine,' I said impatiently. 'You've got two minutes. What do you need to talk to me about so urgently?'

She gestured to my computer. 'I've just sent you an email, Jazz. It's about my contract. Before I fly to England I wanted us to . . . review it.'

I smelled trouble. The fact that she'd emailed me, even though she also intended to come into my office meant that it was a matter she wanted in writing. The fact that she'd brought this matter up the day before an important work trip was also no coincidence. She thought she had me over a barrel; if I said no to whatever demand she was going to make, she knew it was too late to send another Bee to England. No junior employee could prep for this shoot, not to mention the meetings with the editors, in less than twenty-four hours. I needed Rosa . . . and she knew it.

I clicked open my inbox. Rosa's email was right on the top of my virtual pile, which meant she'd hit 'send' seconds before stalking into my office.

Dear Jasmine,

As you know, I adore working for Queen Bee. I think you're a boss in a million and believe that I have proved myself as a reliable, loyal and dedicated employee and a crucial and intrinsic member of the team.

I am however concerned that I am not being paid adequately for the extra hours I put in at the office. My contract states that I am expected to work eight hours a day, six days a week, but this does not take into account the lunch breaks I work through, the after-work events I attend and the Saturdays when I pop in to access the blogging database.

As such, I would like to be remunerated in fifteen-minute increments instead of a day rate. All the extra fifteen minutes that I work quickly add up and I believe that by calculating my wage this way, I will be paid more accurately and not be undervalued.

I thank you for your cooperation in this matter.

Warm regards,
Rosa

It took me a few moments to digest what I was reading. She wanted to be paid in what? Fifteen-minute increments? Had the radiation from her iPhone addiction addled her brain?

Everyone knows that the hours laid out in your contract are underestimated. You don't pursue a job in PR if you want to clock off at 5 pm. As for lunch breaks, you might not get a dedicated window to eat a sandwich, but this time is made up in kind. The Bees might think I'm an idiot, but I know that not all the 'business meetings' they leave the office for are legit. When a Bee goes out to meet a client and comes back with different-coloured nail polish and a blow-dry it's not hard to guess she told a little white lie. However, I'm a fair boss and I overlook it, as long as they don't take the mickey. Yet here was Rosa doing just that.

'My love, I am not going to pay you in fifteen-minute increments,' I told her. 'It's just out of the question and I'm insulted you even ask me. Do you know what the other Sydney PR companies pay their rookies? A whole lot less than I pay you, I assure you.'

Rosa shuffled her feet, clad in the latest Miu Miu sneakers, which had been a gift from me when the Queen Bee Instagram feed cracked 70,000 followers. 'I've read up about my legal rights, Jasmine,' she said, sounding less and less sure of herself. 'If I really wanted to I could sue you for the additional hours I've worked up till now and the stress caused by the depletion of my free time. I could sue you for breaching my human rights.'

That last sentence didn't really even make sense, but Rosa clearly thought it sounded impressive. That's the problem with the internet these days. Just as you can google a headache and convince yourself you have five types of cancer, you can also google 'workplace discrimination' and think you have a case worthy of *Law & Order*.

As I sat there trying to think of a polite way of telling Rosa to take a hike, she took matters into her own hands. 'I'm sorry, Jasmine, but if you don't agree to my very fair requirements I'm going to have to suspend my employment while I seek legal advice. Of course, that means I won't be able to go to London, so the photo shoot will probably have to be cancelled. And Stitched won't be happy. How much is their contract worth? Isn't it $60,000 . . . ?'

She let that figure hang in the air. Pleeease! I do not give in to blackmail. I didn't even need to weigh up whether to give in to her demands. Imagine the example it would set to the other Bees if I started paying her in quarter-hour segments. Would I subtract fifteen minutes every time she visited the bathroom, or logged onto Skype to wave at her boyfriend?

Okay, sometimes I do check my employees' internet history. What? The office computers are my property. Rosa's most-visited websites were Skype and Snapchat. She didn't need either for Queen Bee business so I assumed they were for extracurricular activities. Her boyfriend was probably the one advising her to ask for a pay rise. Well, he was going to be very disappointed when his girlfriend called to update him.

Without another moment's thought, I picked up the phone on my desk and dialled through to reception. 'Lulu, please can you fetch a cardboard box for Rosa and leave it on her desk.' My assistant knew my code by now. A request for a cardboard box means 'another one bites the dust'.

You might think I'm ruthless, but I don't have any loyalty to these kids if they don't have any loyalty to me. I also had to protect the other members of the Queen Bee team. An employee with a negative attitude is like a virus, infecting the rest of the hive and dragging down morale. It was clear from Rosa's actions that she was not a team player, as she was leaving us in the shit by pulling this stunt the day before her London trip. The collaboration between Savannah and Stitched was the biggest deal we'd struck since starting The Talent Hive. It was part of a twelve-month contract that would see Savannah's face on billboards and bus stops all across Australia. Every Bee knew that if the client wasn't happy we wouldn't win new business. There was a lot to lose on this one.

Yet Rosa was only looking out for number one. Well, good luck and good riddance. Let her go to a rival publicity company. I knew for a fact that the girls at Wilderstein PR were not paid nearly as generously as my Bees. They were certainly not gifted designer handbags, Mercedes Coupés and a fully loaded trip to Glastonbury.

In the early days of Queen Bee, five years ago, I hired a girl called Holly who I then had to fire after it became clear she was a kleptomaniac. She had been stealing samples from the office, not to mention money from my wallet. I'll never forget it, as it was quite the fraught farewell. In fact, it ended in police escorting Holly out of the building after a punch-up (this is not a common occurrence in my office!).

Since then I had been waiting to see where Holly would pop up next and if she'd try to steal my clients (this is a common occurrence). But the twenty-eight-year-old seemed to have taken a very early retirement. She'd started dating a professional soccer player and become a full-time, fully bankrolled WAG, with the hair extensions to go with the stereotype. In a way, I thought it was a waste. Okay, she was crazy, but she was also a talented publicist – if only she hadn't been a thief as well.

Then, one morning, I clicked onto *The Sun* homepage and was confronted with Holly's photograph, under the headline 'SOCIALITE ON TRIAL'. The sticky-fingered publicist had been caught with – according to the papers – a dozen fake credit cards under other people's names. It seems she'd risen from pickpocket to (failed) fraudster since leaving stable employment.

I have a friend in the Sydney police force who forwarded me Holly's mug shot to give me a giggle. She was wearing the same guilty expression as she had when I'd spotted her in the social pages of *The Sun* wearing a one-of-a-kind Allison Palmer dress which had gone missing from our showroom the week before.

I knew I shouldn't laugh at her arrest, but I did. Karma is a bitch and always comes around in the end. The problem is that many PR apprentices seem to think they're invincible. It's the Gen Y stereotype; many are over-privileged and think they're owed a living, rather than needing to work for one like the rest of us. But people in this town have very long memories, so these young girls should be more careful who they screw over. Still, after paying Rosa for her four-week notice period she would no longer be my problem.

Now I just had to figure out who to send to Glastonbury in her place.

15

As Shelley and I settled into our first-class seats, the pilot greeted us over the tannoy: 'Welcome to your flight to London Heathrow. The flight time is twenty-three hours and thirty minutes. We hope you enjoy your journey.'

Yes, I'd fixed the Glastonbury situation in the best way I knew how – by sending myself. Well, what other choice did I have? I couldn't prep another Bee in time, and this contract was too important just to wing it. So as soon as Rosa had been escorted from my office, I made two phone calls. The first was to Shelley to see if she fancied a long-haul adventure. Of course she did, once I threw in the words 'Harrods' and 'Harvey Nichols summer sale'. I also thought about inviting Tara, but decided that Shelley and I could do with some one-on-one time, as I had been slightly neglecting her recently.

The second call was to my husband: 'Hey bud, how's your schedule looking for the next five days? Busy? Well, I need you to do some imaginative reshuffling. Fifi's your baby too.' I'd taken the brunt of the baby work for the past few months and now it was time to pass the baton. See, buddy, you're not the only one with transatlantic commitments!

I usually prefer to take Fifi on my work trips, but Glastonbury isn't a place for a two-year-old. I'd thought about taking her: it would certainly be an education, and I could get her some of those cute noise-cancelling earphones I always see Lila Grace Moss and Apple Paltrow wearing at concerts. But that wouldn't shield her eyes from the vices that are inevitably on display at any festival. I didn't want to have to explain why the girl in the floral headdress was napping in a puddle or why that man wearing a tiger onesie was handing around little white sweeties. It was far better that I leave Fifi in the hands of her father. It would be a good bonding experience for them. And it's not like he'd have to quit his day job, as he'd still have the nanny on hand to help him.

Michael scoffed when I told him about the trip. 'You and Shelley . . . at Glastonbury? You do know it's notorious for raining every year, so you'll be waist deep in mud and sleeping in a tent. It's a long way from your suite at the Four Seasons.'

I knew that. I'm not a total festival novice. But it was Michael who was behind the times. Didn't he know that Glasto has gone glam? As our plane started its ascent, and Shelley poured her third glass of champagne ('We have to keep hydrated'), I pulled out my iPad to show her the photographs of our festival digs.

When I realised that I would have to take Rosa's place on the trip, I immediately upgraded both the flight and the accommodation. When my staff go on work trips I send them economy. Well, I'm not made of money, and I do send them off with a care package that includes sleeping pills and a neck pillow. But I don't do cattle class. I'm not a snob: I just choose to be comfortable. A friend of mine who is a fashion designer put it perfectly: 'Honey, we work like fucking dogs. I'd rather chew my own nuts off than be trapped in a big metal box with those losers for twenty-odd hours.' He now only flies by private jet. I actually quite like commercial flights. At least there's the duty-free, plus you never know who you might end up sitting next to. On my last trip to LA I'd been 'pod partners' with Russell Brand, who gave me a peek at the novel he was writing. You never know when a long-haul flight will turn into a networking opportunity.

I'd also upgraded the accommodation. Originally Rosa was going to be staying at the Radisson in Covent Garden and then a teepee at Glasto. As accommodation goes, they were fine, but I wanted fabulous. Shelley and I were now booked into the Bulgari Hotel in Knightsbridge for the first night of our trip. I had a jam-packed day of business meetings in the city, and then we'd follow the fleets of hippies to the festival, where we'd be meeting Savannah and the crew for the Stitched photo shoot. But we wouldn't be slumming it with the other happy campers; there was no way Shelley would have agreed to come if I'd said the words 'tarpaulin' and 'sleeping bag'.

'Check this out,' I told Shelley, proffering her my iPad, which showed a photograph of a tent fit for an Arabian princess, with sweeping silk curtains and real roses growing around the doorway. We would be staying in a five-star 'pop-up hotel' that was being erected for the first time on the edge of the Glastonbury site. It had been described as 'The Ritz of Glampsites', and consisted of 138 tents. But these weren't tents as you or I remember from Girl Scouts. The poshest tent – the Treehouse suite – cost over $10,000 for the long weekend, and had four double beds, three bathrooms, Persian rugs on the floor and antique furniture. It also had a butler on hand to cater for the guests' every whim (champagne the night before and iced Earl Grey tea and scones the morning after. How very British!). I'd tried to book the Treehouse suite for Shelley and me, but apparently Beyoncé and Jay-Z beat me to it . . .

The good news was that our tent was only slightly less luxurious. As well as a flat-screen television it had free wi-fi, electric heating and air-conditioning (not that I expected to need that in England). Our canvas castle was also conveniently close to the 'spa tent' where festival-goers could book in for a massage, pedicure or facial. It seemed a waste to even leave to listen to the music.

As Shelley flicked through the photos, nodding in approval, she also had a surprise for me. I had booked a private chauffeur to drive us the four hours from London to the festival, but Shelley had been doing her own research. 'Nobody who is anybody drives to Glastonbury,' she exclaimed, sloshing her champagne as we hit a patch of turbulence. 'Do you really want to be stuck in a traffic jam with thousands of beer-swilling revellers? Oh no, darling, we're arriving in style . . .' Unbeknown to me, my best friend had booked a private helicopter to shuttle us from London to a heli-pad down the road from the festival. According to rumours, Justin Timberlake would also be choppering in the same morning as us. Now I was really starting to get excited. I felt like a freaking rock star. After the last few months, this was exactly the adventure I needed.

Plus, the bigwigs at Stitched were delighted that I'd made the effort to fly to London to oversee their photo shoot rather than sending a rooky. It was a win-win situation and I was suddenly very happy that I'd taken on the task myself. It would be fun. What could possibly go wrong?

It seems I'd overlooked one rogue factor . . . Savannah Jagger. I knew she could be difficult, but over the next week she surpassed all of my worst expectations. I should have predicted the blogger would be a handful after she'd thrown a tantrum when we booked her tickets because she couldn't bring her dog over with her from Sydney. I had to explain the term 'quarantine'.

That was just the first strop of many. She was a punish and a half. Don't be fooled by her smiley-faced Instagram photos, this girl is a living nightmare. By the end of the trip, it felt like an out-of-body experience.

It all started before Savannah even landed in London. I had lined up an interview with a reporter from the *Daily Mail*, who wanted to talk to Savannah about how she'd become an Instagram icon (she has 500,000 followers and counting). It was a great opportunity for the fashion blogger and was only happening because I'd called in a favour with their showbiz editor, Minky Barton. When Kate and Wills were visiting Australia I'd helped her out with a scoop by getting her an interview with the Sydney hair stylist who gave the duchess a fringe trim. That kind of insider knowledge carries a lot of currency.

I'm not sure that Savannah really appreciated the opportunity. When I emailed her to line up an interview time, she replied, 'The *Daily Mail*? Can't we get *Grazia* magazine instead?' She then uttered the two words every journalist dreads – copy approval. 'You can tell them I'll only do the interview if they send through the questions in advance for me to approve,' she huffed. 'I don't want to be put on the spot and made to look stupid. I know how these journalists work. I've watched *How to Lose Friends & Alienate People*.'

I tried to convince her that she didn't have anything to worry about. This was a light-hearted article (I nearly said 'puff piece' but caught myself at the last minute) and they wouldn't have any hidden agenda. They just wanted to hear about her clothes, her favourite shopping spots, and the power of social media. It wasn't an undercover investigation.

But she was adamant. 'If I don't see the questions I won't do the interview. And I won't talk about my private life, how much money I earn or how much money I spend. It's none of their fucking business.'

This would leave the journalist with very little to work with. I wondered what Savannah was hiding. She wouldn't be the first blogger to be drowning in debt, living the high life on a pile of overburdened credit cards.

This phone conversation took place while I waited in the customs line at Heathrow Airport. Savannah was about to board her own plane at Sydney and her last words to me were, 'Make it happen or I'm pulling out of the interview.'

I waited until Shelley and I had checked in to the Bulgari and been shown to our suite before booting up my laptop and emailing Minky. She was not going to be happy. Every journalist I know hates sending questions in advance of an interview, because it makes the conversation stilted. They can't go with the flow if they're locked down to bullet points. Also, no one likes to be told how to do their job.

As expected, Minky's response was seriously pissy.

From: MBarton@mailonline.co.uk
To: Jasmine@Queenbee.com
Subject: Re: Savannah Jagger the superstar blogger
I don't mean to sound·like a bitch, Jasmine, but are you kidding me? I spent this morning interviewing P. Diddy and he didn't ask for a list of interview questions, and yet this little blogger wants special treatment. This is ridiculous.

I have never, ever sent through a list of interview questions before the event in my life, and I'm slightly offended that you'd even ask me to. I lined up the interview with Savannah because you're a friend and I wanted to make the story happen, but I can just as easily find another fashion blogger to interview. I have Rumi Neely from Fashion Toast on speed dial and she's in town for Glastonbury too.

You need to tell your dear Savannah that she needs to seriously rethink the way she deals with the media. She's a public figure now and there are going to be questions about her private life. I just looked at her Instagram feed and there are photos of her snogging her boyfriend, with full tongues on show, and pictures of her playing volleyball topless. You can't tell me this girl is shy and worried about her reputation.

Err, sorry to rant. Feel free to forward this email directly to Savannah, as she's the one I have the issue with. I still love you, Jazzy Lou. As usual, you've been nothing but helpful and amazing. But you do need to get your blogger to toe the line. This girl is a lampshade: you feel less bright just being in the room with her!

Minky x

P.S. We'll pass on the interview for now, thanks. It just isn't worth the effort from our end.

P.P.S. Could you get me an interview with Miranda Kerr? Now I would LOVE to talk with her.

I groaned out loud when I read Minky's response. Although she wasn't blaming me, it certainly wasn't a win for me professionally. Damn it. I closed the leather cover of my iPad case with a snap and threw it onto the bed, where it bounced off the mountain of scatter cushions and fell onto the floor.

'What's up?' asked Shelley. 'You look as if you've just heard that Fashion Week is cancelled.' My travel buddy was sitting at the dressing table, clad in the hotel's complimentary silk robe, flicking through a brochure for the gym on the top floor.

'Oh, you know, the usual,' I sighed. 'A battle of the egos between semi-celebrities and journalists. I wish they could all just play happily together and realise they need each other. I feel like a diplomat sometimes, trying to get everybody to compromise.'

Shelley picked up an apple from the complimentary fruit bowl and threw it at my head. 'You know what you need, Jazzy Lou? A workout! That'll get you in a better headspace.'

To my amazement, our kiddie yoga class had triggered a health kick in my friend, who was now dropping into conversation phrases like 'resistance training' and 'calorie expenditure'. She'd started going to a yoga class every morning with a muscle-bound teacher called Keenan who had a reputation for being very 'handsy'. If I didn't know better, I'd say Shelley was prowling for a partner.

Whatever her motivation, all the exercise was paying off. The previous week she'd called me in happy hysterics because she'd bought a size ten dress – and had actually fitted into it. She'd even started mixing her champagne with orange juice, and swapped her vodka and Coke for vodka and tonic. For Shelley this was serious progress.

Despite the jetlag migraine throbbing at my temples, a visit to the gym actually wasn't a bad suggestion. I very much doubted that a workout would cheer me up, but a session of celebrity spotting might help. I happened to know that the gym at the Bulgari Hotel was frequented by London's most famous fitness fanatics. It's run by celebrity trainer James Duigan, who honed the bods of Rosie Huntington-Whiteley, Jennifer Lawrence, and Australia's most luscious export, Elle Macpherson. The gym is so exclusive that to be a member you have to submit an application to a board, who judge whether you're of high enough calibre to join.

It's a sign of the times that it's now harder to get into a gym than it is to get into the VIP area of Mahiki when Prince Harry is in the nightclub. But despite the super-tight security, hotel guests got a free pass. They must assume that, if you can afford to stay there, you're not a ragamuffin or a troublemaker.

So Shelley and I grabbed our gym kit and made our way to the elevator for the gym, which was constantly manned by a security guard with a gun-shaped bulge in his jacket.

The fitness centre was split into two sections: a large area filled with shiny machines, and a smaller room with one-way mirrored glass. 'What's in there?' I asked the gym instructor on duty, pointing to the closed door of the small room.

'Oh, that's the personal training room,' he replied, handing me a bottle of water. 'It's also where we train guests who need a little more . . . privacy.'

Ah, so that's where all the high-profilers sweat. Shelley and I exchanged intrigued glances. She knew what I was thinking. Imagine who could be behind that very door right now, being put through their paces on the elliptical trainer.

'Can we have a tour?' asked Shelley. 'I'm interested in booking a personal training session and would like to see if the equipment is . . . adequate.'

The instructor looked shifty. 'Sorry, madam, but that room is currently occupied with a special guest. Usually I would say yes but they have asked not to be disturbed.'

This was the worst thing he could have said around someone with an imagination like mine. There was no way I was moving until I knew who was inside there. My mind went into overdrive, running through a list of the Brit-pack: Pippa Middleton, Kate Winslet, Keira Knightley? I could do with signing a British A-lister to The Talent Hive. That would really elevate us to another level.

On the very rare occasion that I visit the gym I usually get bored within ten minutes and slink off to the sauna. But after positioning myself on a treadmill facing the door of the VIP room, I then embarked on the longest workout of my life. There was no way I was moving until I saw who was in there. There was only one door out . . . and I'd be waiting on the other side of it.

After seventy minutes of fast walking (I do not run), my leg muscles were screaming and I was covered in sweat. The gym instructor was starting to shoot me worried looks. 'Um, madam, maybe we should swap to the mats and do some gentle stretching?'

But the stretching area was hidden behind a screen. I wasn't going to interrupt my view now. And then, finally, the handle of the VIP door shook and it creaked open. Yes, YES! My marathon walking session had been worth it. I had out-exercised the celebrity.

The first person out of the room was a personal trainer, a long-limbed girl with a swinging ponytail, carrying a clipboard. And behind her walked the celebrity . . . Oh, bloody hell, you must be kidding me.

It was Rumi Neely from Fashion Toast, dressed in a Mary Katrantzou psychedelic sweater and Acne shorts (even her gym kit was mega stylish). The very special person who couldn't possibly share a gym with mere mortals was a freaking fashion blogger. Was there no escaping them?

As Rumi sashayed past me, I hit the stop button on my treadmill and hobbled after her to the changing room. When she was in the shower I slipped my business card into her gym bag. I didn't really need – or want – another fashionista for The Talent Hive, but I'm also never one to let an opportunity pass me by.

Like them or loathe them, right now bloggers had the power.

16

From the moment Savannah arrived on the photo shoot I knew she was going to cause trouble. Well, I should say from the moment Savannah almost *didn't* arrive. The call time was 5 am, because we had to drive for three hours from London to a property in Oxford where the shoot was taking place. Although it was a Glastonbury-themed shoot, it wasn't actually taking place at Glasto because we hadn't been able to get permission. This was probably a good thing anyway, as trying to get the perfect shot when you're surrounded by thousands of chemically enhanced revellers is not the easiest situation (I'd learned this the hard way after a disastrous shoot with a girl band at Coachella).

The plan was for the crew to meet at 5 am outside the Bulgari; from there, we'd drive out into the countryside in convoy. Savannah was also staying at our hotel, although our paths hadn't crossed since she'd flown in the previous morning. I'd had an early night to prepare for getting up with the birds, but from Savannah's Instagram page she'd gone with the opposite strategy. At 2 am she posted an Instagram video showing her in Annabel's nightclub in Mayfair, dancing with the British aristocrat Arthur Landon (Prince Harry's bestie who was in Las Vegas during the notorious naked-video incident). At the same time Savannah also sent me a text: 'Babes, I won't be seeing you at 5 am. I'll see you at 7 am instead. Thanks babes. See yas.'

Luckily I sleep with my iPhone in my right hand like a comfort blanket (it's a habit Michael hates), so I was woken up by the vibrations. Um, no Savannah, that is not okay. The call time was 5 am and it was immovable. We had an entire team – photographer, stylists, makeup artist and three assistants – meeting then because we had a huge day ahead of us. Who did she think she was – Kate Moss?

'Sorry, Savannah, but the call time can't be any later than 5 o'clock,' I texted back. 'We need all the time we can get as we have ten looks to shoot while the light is good. See ya bright and early.'

My volatile model didn't reply – she was probably too busy downing Arthur's favourite drink, the Christian's Cannon cocktail, a mix of rum, Guinness, maple syrup and a bottle of champagne served in a lit cannon. It made my stomach churn even to think about it.

A lot of top models work hard and party even harder. That's why a makeup artist's kit always contains Nurofen, Berocca, and perfumed hairspray to hide the booze smell. Their hangovers are overlooked, and red eyes are Photoshopped out, because it's seen as a trait of the profession. But it isn't okay to hold up an entire shoot because you've missed your bedtime.

I was not going to let Savannah lie down (or lie in) on the job. I called down to reception and ordered her a wakeup call for 4.40, 4.45, 4.50 and 4.55. That should do it. I just hoped that Savannah would make it back to her bedroom that night and not have a spontaneous sleepover with a Sloaney. I know how charming those boys from Eton can be with their chat-up lines: 'Do you want to come back to my dorm room and see my rowing boat . . . ?'

The rest of the night I tossed and turned, imagining the fallout from Stitched if Savannah didn't appear and we missed our window. We only had one day to shoot Savannah before Glastonbury began. After that, she wasn't contractually our responsibility and could go off the rails as much as she wanted.

To my relief, Savannah did make it back to her own bed – but she proved almost impossible to pry out of it. In the end I had to send the driver to knock on her door (for ten minutes). I figured a seven-foot chauffeur would be far more intimidating than a petite publicist – even if my morning face is pretty scary.

When Savannah finally crawled into the car eighty minutes late, she clearly didn't recognise me, even though we'd had a two-hour meeting when I'd signed her to The Talent Hive.

I assure you I hadn't changed my appearance since then, or in the past decade (if it ain't broke then don't fix it). As the fashion blogger slumped in the back seat, slugging on a bottle of Lucozade Max, she peered at me from under her baseball cap. Her eyes were sunken and she had a cold sore we'd have to Photoshop out. Her mood was as fiery as her complexion. 'Who are YOU?' she snapped. 'Are you the one who brought the clothing?'

She was right in a sense. I had lugged four suitcases of Stitched samples onto the plane with me. Thank god I have friends in high places and could flout the baggage allowance (I was like a smuggler of sweaters). From that moment on, Savannah assumed I was a fashion assistant. In her eyes, I was just a low-level flunky and therefore her personal slave for the day.

Before I could correct her (I'm your publicity manager, remember?), she pulled out her iPod, jammed in her earphones and spent the next three hours staring out the window. She only broke her silence to call her boyfriend, who didn't seem to be able to get a word in. The one-sided conversation went like this: 'Did you see my latest Instagram pics, babes? Did you like my hair? Did you like my shoes? Doesn't my new spray tan make my hair pop!'

I'd met her boyfriend Scott once before, when we'd been seated together at a David Jones fashion show where Savannah had been given backstage access to write about the new collection. We'd only spent forty-five minutes together, but in that time I decided he was the nicest guy I'd ever met, polite, sweet and humble. He works in IT and seemed so out of place in the fashion scene – which I mean as a compliment. He was a stark contrast to Savannah. I felt sorry for him, especially if the rumours about her sleeping with a string of male photographers behind his back were true. It's a cliché, but photographers get no shortage of nooky. Something about having a camera around their neck seems to transform any man into a sex symbol in the eyes of a model.

It was funny that Savannah didn't recognise me – because the photographer and stylist didn't recognise her either. Here's the thing, if you look on Savannah's Instagram feed she appears practically anorexic. In every photograph her legs come up to her armpits and you could wrap your hands around her waist. Her figure is very London Fashion Week, which was one of the reasons why Stitched was so interested in hiring her. When we were preparing for the photo shoot, she'd emailed over her measurements (waist: 24, hips: 32, bust: 28, dress size: 4). And the week before the trip, she'd posted a photograph on Instagram of a line of juice bottles, labelled one to six: 'Countdown to Glastonbury begins with a detox. #cleanse.'

Well, maybe the long-haul flight had made her retain water or maybe she balloons when she's on her period. Or maybe she's just a liar. Because when Savannah arrived she was . . . well, not fat, but not skinny either. There was absolutely no way she was going to fit the samples Stitched had sent over.

I discovered later that Savannah uses an app called Liquify, which lets you slim down your social media photos. It's like

Instagram liposuction, and lets you push, pull, plump or thin any area of an image. That's why she's always standing sideways in her Instagram shots, because that's the easiest angle to stretch without looking fake.

Whatever she does in her free time is her business, and I don't want to judge, but the problem was that Savannah had dreams of moving into modelling. She kept pushing me to line up photo shoots with brands like Stitched – which meant her body was her currency. Did she not understand she'd be caught out as soon as we saw her in the flesh . . . and realised there was more of it than we'd thought?

'Um, is that really Savannah?' whispered the photographer, Bryony Gilbert. We were very lucky to have her. The street styler extraordinaire is a modern-day Helmut Newton, having shot everyone from Naomi Campbell to George Clooney and Michelle Obama. As a favour to me, Bryony had flown in from New York (she'd recently moved there from Melbourne). And how did I repay her? With a chubby model with an attitude problem. I pulled an apologetic face. We were just going to have to make the most of it.

Our base camp for the day was Hadlow Manor in Kent, owned by Lord and Lady Hadlow, and set in the grounds of a huge country estate (you might recognise it from *Downton Abbey*). We'd set up a makeshift dressing room in the library, where I erected a hanging rail and set about steaming the creases out of the samples. This only added to the impression that I was just a fashion assistant, which meant that Savannah didn't try to hide her bad attitude from me.

I couldn't believe the way she spoke to the stylist, especially when the realisation dawned that she wasn't going to be able to fit into any of the clothes provided. Rather than admitting that she may have underestimated her measurements, she blamed Stitched for sending the wrong sizes. 'I can't believe they did this. What a FUCK-UP.' She also hated all the clothes. 'I am not wearing THAT or THAT. I want to wear my OWN jeans and my OWN trainers.'

The poor stylist had to patiently explain that the point of a photo shoot is to promote a label's clothes, and that wearing her old, wornout Genetics would not go down too well with Stitched. It turned into a colossal argument, but in the end Savannah admitted defeat and put on the outfits we'd chosen. First, though, the stylist had to fetch a pair of scissors and cut down the back of all the shorts, so she could squeeze into them.

When she was in hair and makeup her mood didn't get any better. 'I WANT hair extensions!' she yelled at Elise, the makeup artist. 'And give me false lashes. No, bigger than those . . . I said BIGGER.'

She was texting frantically the entire time, holding her phone in front of her face, which made Elise's job even harder. Then she looked up and caught my eye. 'I'm hungry. You, fashion assistant, can you get me some M&Ms?'

I was itching to point out that she probably should lay off the candy when her shorts were already held together with safety pins, but instead I fetched the bowl of sweets from the catering table.

I couldn't quite believe what happened next. Savannah proceeded to open her mouth and tilt back her head. She wanted me to hand-feed her! What's more, I did it. What can I say, I'm an accommodator. Also, I didn't want to rock the boat. I just wanted to get the job done and get out of there. She could think I was the fashion assistant for all I cared; my ego could handle it.

You couldn't make this shit up. There was Savannah, sitting in the makeup chair with two free hands, having her hair brushed by Elise, while the most prestigious publicist in Sydney placed M&Ms on her tongue. I'm surprised she didn't ask me to move her jaw up and down. Chewing is such an effort!

I wish I could say the day got easier from there, but it didn't. When Savannah had been complaining about the 5 am wakeup call, she'd argued that we couldn't possibly need a full day to do the job. 'Oh, babes, I shoot things so quickly,' she'd boasted. 'We'll have this wrapped up by lunchtime. I'm a one-take wonder.'

Well, we were still shooting at ten o'clock at night. In front of a camera, Savannah had all the charisma of a pork chop. On Instagram she looks like a professional poser, but that must be because she just sticks to her most flattering angle. The photographer and I exchanged glances as she repeated the same pose again and again (side on, looking over her shoulder). When I tried to suggest that she mix it up a little, she barked, 'You're just the fashion assistant, what do you know?'

She also thought I was her social media officer, and expected me to take all her behind-the-scenes photographs for Instagram.

I emailed one of the photographs to my contact at Stitched so they could promote the shoot on their own Instagram page. When Savannah was tagged in their photograph, she went ballistic. 'Who the fuck is posting photographs of me on social media without my permission? This is meant to be a closed shoot. What stalker is spying on me?'

I wanted to kick her at this moment. That stalker is the client, you freaking idiot. We wasted so much time that day, stopping intermittently for Savannah to throw her temper tantrums. When working with models, you can usually put their mood swings down to malnourishment, but Savannah's constant food demands put paid to that theory. 'Babes, can you fetch me some activated almonds? Can you peel me an orange? Can you get a straw for my cola, and hold it to my mouth for me? I don't want to smudge my lip gloss.'

By the final look we were all utterly exhausted. Unusually for Britain, it had been a steady thirty degrees all day and there hadn't been any shade. The crew and I were tired, hungry and sunburnt. I'd been up since 4 am. I'd been Savannah's assistant and her skivvy; fed her sweeties and cut her shorts so she could fit her fat arse into them. I was starting to lose my patience.

For the last shot, Savannah had to recline on the bonnet of a vintage open-backed truck, dressed in frayed denim shorts, a checked shirt and an elaborate Indian headdress. The look was 'Daisy Duke goes to Glasto'. It was my favourite outfit of the day, but Savannah had a face like thunder.

At one stage, she thumped the bonnet of the truck with her fist. 'I'm *sooo* parched, I'm dehydrating. Someone needs to get me some water.'

The rest of the crew had their hands full with cameras and lighting, so I volunteered to run back to the house and get some refreshments. When I returned and handed Savannah a bottle of water, she took a huge gulp, then her eyes bulged . . . and she spat it back out all over me. The water sprayed all over the front of my Givency t-shirt, ran down the front of my jeans and all over my shoes. The crew's mouths fell open in shock.

'This water is HOT!' screamed Alexa. 'I asked for COLD water. If I wanted warm water I'd have PISSED in a BOTTLE.' If only her 500,000 Instagram fans could have seen her now, ranting and raving like a fishwife.

That was the moment I hit my limit – as did the photographer, who called it a wrap. Maybe I should have pulled Savannah up on her behaviour but I was too stunned. Also, her behaviour was so erratic that it was actually quite funny. She hadn't won any friends among the crew. She'd had the opportunity to work with the most talented photographer in the UK, and had made herself look like an idiot.

If we didn't get the shots for Stitched then Savannah would just have to lose the contract. It would serve her right for being a total nightmare. I couldn't stand to be around her for another minute. Luckily, at lunchtime I'd made a sneaky call to the car-hire firm and asked them to send another vehicle so that Savannah could be driven back to London on her own.

The drivers were running ten minutes late, so the crew and I had time to clear up after ourselves, wash the dishes and straighten the furniture. It's always good etiquette when you borrow someone's house for a shoot to leave it exactly as you found it. I always send flowers to the homeowner the next morning too. It's these little touches that make Queen Bee stand out from the crowd.

Instead of helping, Savannah disappeared, which was not surprising. Can you imagine the strop if I'd asked her to rinse out our teacups? I found her accidentally when I walked into the library to pack my mountain of garments back into their suitcases . . . and caught her shoving samples into her bag. Ah, so the blogger was a thief as well as a diva. She blushed bright red when I busted her with her hands full of $20 t-shirts – the same t-shirts that she'd previously called ugly and had to be forced into wearing.

'I'm sorry, Savannah,' but I have to return every sample to Stitched,' I said politely. 'However, I'm sure they'll be thrilled to hear you like the clothes so much, and could give you a media discount for the items you'd like to purchase. I wouldn't insult you by giving them to you for free. I know free gifts don't sit well with you ethically.'

As Savannah pulled the t-shirts back out of her bag, I also noticed she'd stashed a box of teabags from the kitchen, a bunch of bananas, and two bottles of hair spray from the makeup artist's kit. As someone who flaunts her high-end handbags and designer shoe-drobe, you'd think she'd be above petty theft.

I've had some difficult days in my career — we once had a shooting at a Converse media event, although that's another story — but the photo shoot with Savannah was up there with my top ten 'wow' moments.

By the time I finally got back to the Bulgari, where I found Shelley asleep under a pile of Harvey Nichols carrier bags, I was delirious with exhaustion and suffering a serious bout of 'post-event depression'. It's always the same after an adrenaline-fuelled assignment. Photo shoots and press events can be so surreal and so exhausting that you don't know which way is up . . . and often fall back to earth with a crash.

I also always have crazy dreams after a day like this, as my brain struggles to process the eccentric characters of the fashion world. That night I dreamed that I was being chased by a chubby blonde driving a fire engine and spraying water from a hose which twirled from the roof of the fire truck like a cowboy's lasso. I woke up drenched in sweat with a throbbing headache that felt like a hangover. God, I was feeling rough . . . and we hadn't even got to the music festival yet.

17

I had been worried that I might look out of place at Glastonbury . . . and I was right. Oh, I fitted in just fine in the lofty confines of the pop-up hotel, but once I was inside the festival grounds, I stuck out like a sore thumb. My signature dress sense isn't exactly bohemian.

Although the photo shoot with Savannah was over, I was still on Queen Bee duty during our stint in the fields of Somerset. On day one of Glastonbury, I was due to meet Bryony the photographer again to take street-style shots of the best-dressed revellers. The top snaps would be used as part of a marketing campaign for The Intersection, the shopping destination in Sydney's Paddington.

You might think shooting street style sounds like a simple assignment, but it can be tricky – not only searching for cute girls but ensuring they sign the release forms and hoping they can remember exactly where they bought every element of their outfit (we'd got in trouble in the past by saying a patent-leather ankle boot was Dolce & Gabbana when it was actually from Target). It's hard enough gathering this information at the best of times, let alone when the girl in question is sloshing a plastic cup of cheap cider and has pupils the size of saucers. But that's Glasto for you!

Predicting that it was going to be a long and highly charged day, I had dressed in an outfit I knew could stand the pace: cropped Chloé pants, a crisp Ralph Lauren shirt and Chanel flats. This fail-safe combo had got me through many a Fashion Week marathon. Even my handbag was practical. While I was at the photo shoot from hell, Shelley had been buying out the high-end shopping mecca of Chelsea (the reality show based on the area was her guilty pleasure), and had picked me up a satchel from Mulberry. You know, the bag that Alexa Chung and her pals all have. She'd even paid extra to have my name embossed on the leather (that's why she's my BFF).

I had packed smart and my satchel contained the survival kit I've perfected for Fashion Week — bandaids, deodorant, phone charger and nail-polish remover wipes (the latter come in handy more often than you'd imagine). I'd also packed a bright red lip gloss, even though I usually only go for nude. I'd read an interview with Poppy Delevingne in which she claimed that a red lippie was her ultimate hangover cure ('It really cheers you up'), and I planned to put it to the test if I did indulge. This was a big if, as I fully intended to be sensible . . .

'Do you think my outfit looks Glasto enough?' I asked Shelley as we shuffled around our tent that morning. A golf buggy would soon pick us up from our front door; all hotel guests were chauffeur-driven the fifty yards to the entrance of the festival. It really was impeccable service.

'You look stellar,' enthused Shelley, who seemed to be going to Glasto in fancy dress – as a Sloane Ranger. She was wearing a pair of Burberry jodhpurs tucked into crocodile-skin Hunter wellies, and a trilby. We were going to a music festival, not a pheasant shoot at a country estate, but who was I to correct her? She'd clearly been reading too many issues of *Tatler*. I was surprised she hadn't accessorised with a riding whip.

Yet I turned out to be the most inappropriately dressed of the pair of us. When it comes to Glastonbury, the dress code seems to be 'cliché'. As we entered the festival gates, flashing our VIP wristbands, I was engulfed in a crowd of clones. When it comes to festival dressing, it seems you just need to follow one simple formula. Cut-off denim shorts with a fringed jacket and/or bag? Check! Suede poncho for cold evenings? Check! Flower hair garlands? Check! Long, tousled hair with a plait and/or feathers? Check! If I took a picture and sepia-filtered it, it could easily pass for Woodstock. In comparison, my front-row outfit made me feel like a nun.

'I seriously need some coffee,' I muttered to Shelley as a girl dressed in a sequinned onesie rolled past us on a skateboard, twirling a fire stick.

Luckily we didn't have to queue at the food stalls for breakfast or lower our taste buds to a bacon and egg sarnie wrapped in polystyrene. I had begged and bartered us access to the VIP area next to the main stage. I instantly felt more comfortable once we left gen public behind us. I feel at home in any area you need to pass through a red rope to access.

No other festival draws quite the same It crowd as Glasto. It's an institution, which is why the tickets sell out in twelve minutes. Shelley and I were goggle-eyed as we entered the VIP section, which was really just a glorified car park with a pavilion at one end that had high partition walls to segregate the important people from the festival hoi polloi.

The decor was . . . interesting. The area was decorated with mini lanterns, kilometres of fairy lights, and sculptures of life-sized animals, from rhinos to giraffes. There was also a Marc Jacobs pop-up store where you could try on the latest shades, and a Hunter wellies boutique selling limited-edition designs, including a pair with a five-inch heel. Shelley had her name on the waiting list without even trying them on.

Although it was only 8 am, the dance floor was filling up quickly and the stars were already arriving. In one corner Carey Mulligan was sipping from a steaming teacup, dressed in an all-black outfit. At the bircher muesli station, Sienna Miller was loading up a bowl with quinoa and almond meal, trying not to dip her fringed sleeve in the yoghurt. I tried not to obviously ogle Cressida Bonas, who was wearing a pair of denim overalls and her signature scrunchie. And was that Florence Welch chasing a man across the dance floor, shouting that she wanted her wellies back? If only cameras weren't banned from the VIP area, this would be Oscar-winning content for the Queen Bee blog.

I couldn't wait until nightfall, when the VIP area was sure to get even rowdier. I have a publicist friend in Palm Springs who oversees the VIP section at Coachella. Last year she texted me all the gossip as it was unfolding. As the cocktails flowed, the celebs turned the area into a playground. Rosie Huntington-Whiteley and Katy Perry went head to head on the volleyball court. Meanwhile, Daisy Lowe got into a ping-pong battle with George Clooney. Who needs sex, drugs and rock 'n' roll?

Unfortunately, we couldn't stay in the VIP sanctuary forever. I had arranged to meet Bryony at 8.30 am by the circus big top so that we could start our street-style search. As we were leaving, we passed Cara Delevingne, wearing denim shorts (of course!) and a fluorescent-yellow shell-suit jacket, with sunglasses in the shape of love hearts. I was starting to feel like a real fuddy-duddy in my smart-casual ensemble.

And I didn't feel any better when we met up with Bryony. She'd obviously got the memo about the festival fashion cliché and was wearing double denim with a paisley headscarf. The first thing she said when she saw me was, 'What are you wearing, Jazzy Lou? You look like you're going to a board meeting. We need to cool you up!'

I looked down at my outfit. This was cool . . . in suburban Sydney. Yet in Bryony's eyes I needed a makeover, and pronto. There was no point in me going back to the hotel, as my suitcase only contained more of the same. We were standing next to the entrance to a pop-up cafe (everything is 'pop-up' these days. Nobody who knows anything says 'temporary'). Grabbing my hand, Bryony pulled me inside the cafe and over to a picnic table in the corner.

'Luckily for you, I have my Glastonbury tool kit,' she exclaimed, unzipping a huge canvas bag with 'Paul's Boutique' stamped on the side. I cringed as she pulled paraphernalia from the pockets – a bag of sequins, a packet of bindis. And was that pink hair dye?

'It's only hair chalk,' insisted Bryony, seeing my worried expression. 'I just rub it in and it washes out. It will only last as long as your hangover, don't worry.'

I was about to protest but then I was distracted by the return of Shelley, who had beein queuing at the food counter for breakfast. I had asked her to get me something healthy – perhaps an egg-white omelette or some porridge. But she'd totally ignored my instructions by the look of her tray, which was weighed down with food that I couldn't even identify.

'What the hell is that?' I asked as Shelley plonked the plates on the table. They smelled like an explosion in Heston Blumenthal's laboratory.

My best friend looked proud of herself. 'They're all the latest London food trends. I thought we should try them all for the authentic Glasto experience. Oh, don't look at me like that, Jazz. You can have freakin' egg-white omelettes at the Four Seasons any day.'

Apparently, I not only had to look like the cool kids but eat like them too. This meant tucking in to bacon sticky buns with date butter, caramelised cauliflower, and a bowl of 'thirty-ingredients noodles' which contained a medley of ingredients including ginger, jalapeno peppers and Nutella. Yes, Nutella! I have to admit it was tastier than it sounds.

'I also got our first round of drinks in,' added Shelley, who seemed to have conveniently forgotten that I was meant to be working. 'I got talking to a guy at the bar who looked exactly like Liam Gallagher . . . in fact, maybe it was him. Anyway, he gave me a quick lesson on hipster cocktails.'

She passed me a jam jar containing a cloudy, fizzy liquid. 'It's called a "Spiced Daisy",' she explained. 'It's tequila, orange curaçao, lime juice, agave nectar and juiced cucumber; also maybe some other stuff but I've forgotten already. I may have downed a drink while I was waiting for the barman to make the others.'

It was a good thing the alcohol had hit my bloodstream by the time Bryony finished her makeover and handed me a pocket mirror. Holy cow! I looked like a hippie who had fallen into a candy-floss machine. My blonde hair was dusted with pink, there were daisies woven into the ends, and I had star-shaped sequins stuck to my cheeks. But I didn't want to sound ungrateful.

'Umm, lovely,' I muttered, as Bryony started laughing.

'Loosen up, Jazz,' she giggled. 'It's not like it's permanent. Anyway, it only looks weird because you're teaming it with that outfit. I've hippied you from the neck up, now we need to transform you from the neck down. Wait right there . . .'

Before I could stop her she was up and running through the crowd, heading towards the cafes. Obediently, I stayed where I was, listening to echoes of Mumford & Sons coming from the nearby stage. Next to me, Shelley was devouring a 'tequila ice-cream sandwich': imagine two gluten-free coconut cookies with tequila-infused ice-cream between them. 'My yoga teacher's gonna kill me,' mumbled Shelley with her mouth full. 'Oh, bugger it. I'm on holiday, and what he doesn't know won't hurt him.'

That was when I noticed a pile of fabric jogging towards us. By the looks of it, Bryony had just bought a market stallholder's entire stock. 'Okay, I may have gone a little overboard,' the photographer laughed, 'but a girl can never have too many tassels . . . or rainbow harems . . . or denim hot pants. Now put these on . . .'

And that's how I found myself at Glastonbury Festival in a mosh pit with 10,000 Kasabian fans, jumping up and down with a glow stick in each hand, yelling at the top of my lungs, 'I feel aliiiiiiiive.' I blame the outfit – there must have been some sort of intoxicating substance in the fabric. I even came up with a name for my alter ego, my hippie twin. 'From now on you have to call me Moonshine,' I insisted to Shelley and Bryony as we queued at the bar for more cocktails.

I don't know whose bright idea it was to take a video of me and Shelley in the VIP tent dancing the Harlem Shake with four members of One Direction, but according to my iPhone record I not only sent the video to Michael . . . but also to Hayden Smith. My husband texted back kind of huffily:

'Well, it looks like you're really missing us.' As for Hayden, he texted back a photograph of himself standing topless in his bathroom. OMG! What had I started?

At some point in the evening, Bryony and I also received a text we weren't expecting – from Savannah Jagger. We found out later that she'd sent the same group message to both of us, the stylist, the makeup artist and the three assistants from the photo shoot. Oh yes, the saga continued,

> I need someone to come to my hotel room right now. I can't get this fucking glue out of my hair. One of you plebs needs to come and do it for me. I TOLD YOU I DIDN'T WANT HAIR EXTENSIONS.

It had actually been Savannah who'd insisted the stylist give her hair extensions, but that had clearly escaped her memory. I remember reading on Savannah's blog that she usually visited the hairdressers three times a week because she hated washing her own hair. Well, I wasn't about to drive four hours back to London to do it for her. It turned out none of the crew answered her SOS text. It was the final straw: she'd have to deal with that first world problem herself.

Anyway, when her text was sent, at 2 am, I was too busy leading an Australia versus England dance-off in the VIP area. On one side was me, Shelley, Jess Hart and Ronan Keating's model girlfriend Storm Uechtritz. On the other side was Henry Holland, Katie Hillier and Pixie Geldof. The Brits were awarded the makeshift trophy (fashioned out of a pint glass covered in tinsel), but I still argue it was a fix, as Elton John was the judge. I knew we should have asked Robert Pattinson to referee it.

By 3 am, the VIP area didn't seem to be winding down but I had drunk myself sober. As I sat slumped in a deck chair massaging my bicep (I think I pulled a muscle doing 'Big Fish, Little Fish'), I heard someone holler my name. 'JASMINE, fancy seeing you here!' I dizzily turned my head to see Cleo Jones, superstar DJ and Aussie export. Following closely behind was her girlfriend (sorry, fiancée) Chelsea Ware, looking ethereal in a white linen dress, which strained over her burgeoning belly.

Chelsea was due any day now. I know because every detail of her pregnancy, from choosing a sperm donor to insemination and ultrasounds, had been documented on her reality TV series *The Bel Air Life*. Love them or hate them, they were cranking up the ratings. It had been nearly two years since the pair met in an elevator at one of my parties; if the relationship was all a publicity stunt as critics claimed, they were certainly playing the long game.

'Jasmine, it's so nice to see you again,' cried Chelsea, who looked suitably more sober than her fiancée. Impending co-parenthood obviously hadn't dampened Cleo's party girl – her eyes were wild and she was waving her arms as if conducting an invisible orchestra. She was also carrying a teapot, pouring liquid straight from the spout into her mouth. Was she channelling Lady Gaga?

'Pssst, Jasmine!' she hissed, beckoning me closer. 'Do you want some tea? It's mushroom flavoured . . . and it's magic!'

Now call me naive but it took me a good few moments to figure out what she meant. 'Umm, no thanks, Cleo. I'm actually thinking of getting to bed soon.' I may be a woman of the world but I've never touched a party drug. I've been on the receiving end of too many cocaine-fuelled monologues by members of Sydney's social set to be tempted by backstreet narcotics. And yes, I realise I sound like a hypocrite. I know I once had a packet of Nurofen pumped from my stomach, but those were pharmaceutical pills and I needed them for medical reasons. Kind of. I don't like the thought of anything bought on the black market – this includes knock-off handbags and illegal substances.

'Go on, Jazzy Lou, have a swig on me,' insisted Cleo. 'It's amaaazzzing. I can see rainbows in my eyeballs. I can hear our unborn baby singing to meeee.'

I glanced at Chelsea to see if she was buying into this bullshit, but she had wandered over to the snack station and was guzzling hot chips out of a paper cone. So much for the trendy food options – even A-listers want a greasy takeaway at the end of a night out.

By this point I just wanted my own bed. My feet were killing me, and I'd misplaced Shelley, who I'd last seen snogging the Liam Gallagher look-alike (who could well have been the real Liam Gallagher. I'd only seen the back of his head). I couldn't believe my best friend had hooked up with someone. This was the first time I'd seen Shelley succumb to a man since we were teenagers. It seemed I wasn't the only one not behaving in their normal manner.

'Cleo, my love, I've gotta go,' I declared, air-kissing her hot cheeks. 'It's been a joy to see you, beautiful. We should catch up for brunch in the morning or something.' I had absolutely no intention of keeping this arrangement but I was confident Cleo wouldn't remember our conversation anyway.

I thought she might try to stop me leaving, but she didn't protest – she did however decide to bid me farewell with a present. 'Well, at least take some with you,' she exclaimed and grabbed the handle of my satchel. The next thing I knew, she'd unclipped the clasp, cocked her teapot and poured the remainder of its contents into my bag. My new Mulberry satchel! In a mark of the handiwork it didn't spill a drop. My lip gloss floated to the surface like a goldfish in a fairground bag.

Seriously, what was it with people tipping liquid over me? I thought the water incident was bad, but at least that wasn't an illegal substance. Call me paranoid, but all I could imagine was a scene of myself walking through the arrivals gate at Sydney airport and being pounced on by a sniffer dog. How would I explain to the customs officials why my bag stunk of hallucinogenic drugs? I'd be one of those jailbirds you read about in the paper who claim they're innocent but nobody believes them.

Suddenly I just wanted to be back in my suburban life with my husband and our daughter, arguing over the fact that he uses my shampoo and leaves his trainers in the hallway. I didn't care that we disagreed on Fifi's bedtime or whether she should be home-schooled. I craved our domestic doldrums. Right then I'd have given anything to be sitting in bed with a takeaway and reading my emails. I wanted my married life back, I wanted to be a wife again . . . but was it too late?

18

The final three days of Glastonbury were far quieter affairs than the first. I spent my days shooting street style with Bryony, and my nights in the chillout tent, where meditation sessions were held and the most raucous activity was a silent disco. I also switched back to my old style of dressing. My alter ego 'Moonshine' was taking early retirement.

Another reason my Glastonbury experience got a whole lot quieter was because I lost Shelley to 'Liam Gallagher' (who was actually a graphic designer called Marcus, but would always be Liam to me). The duo had been inseparable since they locked lips on our first evening. Shelley had even moved into his 'pod pad'. When she opted to sleep in a drafty wooden Wendy house rather than our canvas castle I knew it must be true love. This wasn't just a holiday romance.

This theory was proven on the fourth, and final, day of Glasto when my best friend sent me a text:

Babes, I'm pushing my flight back. I'm going to stay in Blighty for a while. Don't call me crazy! Can't talk yet, don't wanna jinx it. Will call soon. I love you. Shells xoxo.

My flight home to Sydney seemed to take twice as long without a travelling companion. I was desperate to get back and see Michael, who hadn't returned my calls since the drunken text I'd sent him. For the last few days I'd felt like a teenage girl, anxiously checking my phone for news from him, cursing the Somerset fields for having such bad reception.

I tried to pass the flight as best I could. I ate the four-course meal out of boredom, watched seven episodes of How I Met Your Mother and made small talk with Sir Alan Sugar, who was seated in the flatbed next to me. I was bored, bored, bored. So I whiled away the hours imagining a romantic reunion with my husband; he would sweep me into his arms and tell me how much he missed me.

I grabbed the arm of the flight attendant as she brushed past with a tray of buck's fizz. 'Excuse me, could you tell me what date it is?'

'It's the twenty-seventh,' she answered. 'Although you'll land in Sydney the morning of the twenty-eighth because of the time difference.'

My heart sank. FUCK! The deadline for Michael's job decision was the day after tomorrow. In my Glastonbury vortex, time had got away from me. My husband is not the type of person to leave things to the last minute, so he was sure to have made his decision. Nice one, Jazzy Lou. You chose the worst weekend to explore your inner raver. Michael was probably packing for New York right now, while window-shopping Match.com for a more suitable plus one. Maybe a shy and retiring WAG who was more fitting for Park Avenue.

I was exhausted and grumpy by the time we landed in Sydney, despite managing to log a solid few hours' sleep after scoring a sleeping pill from Lord Alan. While waiting for my luggage to appear on the carousel, I turned my iPhone off flight mode and it sprung into life with an impatient beep: 2364 emails and five text messages. READ ME! My technology isn't used to being left waiting.

I read the text from Michael first. See, husband, you are my priority!

Hope you had a safe flight. Fifi is with the nanny at the hotel. I'm swamped at work. See you sometime soon.

Oh, where was Shelley when I needed a girlfriend to help me analyse this message? I knew Michael had probably punched it out while waiting in line for an elevator, but I still pulled each word apart for hidden meanings. He was concerned for my safety – that was a good thing. But he had said 'sometime soon' – what did that mean? Soon as in 'today', or soon as in 'five years' time'? Be clearer, buddy! I couldn't get away with sending a press release that vague.

There was an equally elusive text from my father – the first communication from him since he'd asked me to stash Tessa's diamonds.

Jazzy Lou, can we meet? I need to speak to you about something. It's urgent. Where are you?

I had to sit on my hands to stop myself from snapping back a reply. I needed to think about my options before deciding if I wanted my dad in my life . . . now or ever again.

I temporarily dragged myself away from my iPhone to manhandle the four huge suitcases of Stitched clothing through customs. I held my breath as I passed by the sniffer dogs with their uniformed handlers, but – thank god – the bottle of Diptyque perfume I'd liberally sprayed into my satchel seemed to have covered the stench of Cleo's tea.

When going through security in Heathrow, I had also purposefully latched onto the back of a group of grubby-looking backpackers with marijuana leaves stamped on their backpacks. If the dogs were looking for troublemakers I hoped the boys in front would distract them. Now, as I strolled through customs, trying to look nonchalant, I put my iPhone to my ear and had a fake conversation. 'Hi, darling. Yes, I'll be home for dinner. Meat and two veg would be lovely.' See, officer, I'm just a working mother, not a drugs mule . . .

I had been holding out hope that Michael might be waiting for me at the airport, as I'd texted him my flight details. But as I scanned the faces of the eager relatives at the arrival gate waving 'welcome home' banners, they were all strangers. This never usually bothered me – I'm a practised solo traveller – until today.

Once I was settled in the back of a taxi, I delved into my inbox.

To: Jasmine@Queenbee.com

From: Bryonyphotos@hotmail.com

Subject: Savannah – retouching

Hi Jasmine,

Well, the fun doesn't stop. I just had an email from Savannah's management (isn't this you? Has she sacked you?). Looks like the retouch from the Stitched shoot isn't trim enough for her.

Hmm, what do you think? I'm nervous she's about to have a major spat. Might be better to look like we're accommodating in the short term. I'll retouch even thinner and send you the new pics to look at pronto. It's a fine line between fashion thin and third-world thin, as you and I both know.

Bx

I replied immediately:

To: Bryonyphotos@hotmail.com

From: Jasmine@Queenbee.com

Subject: Savannah – retouching

Hi love,

Whatever you do, DO NOT GO ANY THINNER! I've seen the before and after photos and you've already been more than generous. She won't be satisfied until you can drive a double-decker bus through her thigh gap. We've pandered to her enough. This chick is out of control!

P.S. Can you forward me the email from her 'management'? I was planning to ditch her anyway. I don't care if she has 500,000 fans . . . I am not one of them.

To: Savannah@Daretowear.com
From: Jasmine@Queenbee.com
Subject: Professional courtesy

Hi Savannah,

I'll be candid. I am quite annoyed by the fact that I had to learn from a third party that you had signed up to a second creative management company.

I have invested a lot of time and money in you and Dare to Wear. You are my friend, but to think you can work with two agencies is totally unrealistic – not to mention insulting and unprofessional. I have worked tirelessly on PR and deals for you – and taken a mere 20%.

The events of the past week were, quite frankly, enough for me to halt our relationship immediately and take you off our client list.

I run a professional operation. I am not in a position where I need to be used for bits and pieces of work that suit you. If

I worked like that, believe me, The Talent Hive wouldn't have grown to what it has become in the past six months.

Savannah, we will honour the deals arranged and in progress – Stitched being the main contract – however, beyond that we won't be able to assist.

I am all about loyalty. I have people banging down our door to take them on. I don't need to feel undervalued, unappreciated and mistreated.

Good luck,

Jasmine

I didn't know or care at that point who Savannah's new management was, but I later discovered it was one of her rich girlfriends, who'd just returned from three years spent 'posh packing' around Europe and now wanted to use daddy's money to become a publicist. Never mind the fact that she had zero experience. Too many girls think they can do my job just because they like to party. Just because you like shopping doesn't make you a fashion designer, my love.

Anyway, Savannah did me a favour, as I now had a legitimate reason to shelve her. I'd have looked petty if I sacked her just because she showered me with saliva. This way I sounded professional and could take the high ground. I hoped for Stitched's sake the Glastonbury shoot turned out well, but Savannah could end up on the professional scrapheap for all I cared. I secretly suspected she'd been buying fans on Instagram anyway (on the social media black market you can buy 50,000 fans for just $500). Once Savannah was officially off my books, I might have to give Luke at *The Sun* a nudge. But right now I had 2363 more emails still to get through.

From: JacksonSaunders@interiordelight.com

To: Jasmine@Queenbee.com

Subject: Your Palace Awaits

The project is over: Leonardo da Vinci has completed the Sistine Chapel, David Beckham has scored the final goal, Shane Warne has hit the final wicket . . . and any other metaphors that you can think of. In case you haven't got the gist, I AM FINITO! Your palace awaits you, my darling. It's time for you to move back into your newly decorated abode. My pleasure!

Smooches,

Jackson

P.S. The invoice is in the post in an unmarked envelope. I know you don't want that husband of yours seeing the final figure (uncultured philistine!).

From: GChalmers@Redbuzz.com

To: Jasmine@Queenbee.com

Subject: Introduction – via Hayden Smith

Hi Jasmine,

We haven't met before, but my name is Geoffrey Chalmers and I am the CEO of the energy drink brand Red Buzz. We have just collaborated with the cricketer Hayden Smith on a range of new flavours, including 'baggy green apple' and 'perfect pitch papaya'.

We are planning to launch this new range as a key press event in Melbourne. On the recommendation of several people we would like to speak to you about handling the publicity campaign and press party. In fact, Hayden specifically asked that Queen Bee be the chosen PR firm. He would like you to personally manage the account if possible, although I appreciate that your schedule is probably extremely full.

If this is of interest, please let me know and I'll organise a conference call between you, myself and Hayden. I have to say that usually with celeb collaborations they are silent partners, but Hayden has been refreshingly hands-on.

Cheers for now,

Geoff

After Smithy had sent me the scantily clad photograph of himself, I had made the executive decision not to reply to him – and I certainly wasn't going to take him shopping as he'd originally suggested. But it seemed Smithy was more wily than I'd first suspected. He hadn't been able to capture my emotional attention so was now trying to spark my business interest. It would be a good alignment and a coup for Queen Bee PR. Red Buzz was a major sponsor of the Cricket World Cup, and although sporting events weren't usually my forte, I'd heard they had a $6 million budget to blow. I could become a sports fan with that kind of incentive. But was it safe to work with Hayden Smith? I wasn't so sure I could trust him . . . or myself.

I filed the email, along with the text from my father, in my 'deal with later' folder. My taxi was pulling up outside the Four Seasons anyway. On the way to my room I stopped off at reception and broke the news that they were going to be losing a long-termer. The receptionist, who was new, had to ask my name and then misspelt it as she was searching for my details on the computer. So much for feeling like one of the Four Seasons family: I was just another guest who was only as valuable as her mini-bar bill.

Thankfully, one person was happy to see me. When I unlocked the door of my hotel room, Fifi flung herself at my legs, wiping mushed banana from her mouth onto my Scanlan & Theodore leather leggings. She was delighted with the gifts I'd brought her from London: a stuffed Paddington bear from Hamleys, some toffee bonbons from Selfridges food hall and a pair of glittery pink angel wings from Glastonbury. As her mother's daughter, she immediately started playing, eating and wearing the gifts in unison.

I also had some other good news for my toddler. 'Guess what, Fifi? The first shipment of your fascinators has arrived!' While I was away, Anya had texted me a photograph of the boxes upon boxes of hair bows, and a sample of the range, which looked even cuter than I'd hoped. I'd already tweeted the photograph to Fifi's fans as a teaser:

Aaaah, my #fifisfascinators have landed. So excited to share
them with my friends.

I'd had requests from *Bizarre* magazine, *Grazia* and the
Daily Mail asking for interviews with my teeny entrepreneur
(obviously Minky Barton at the *Daily Mail* had forgiven me
for the Savannah incident). And we'd already had emails from
Fifi fans across the world asking if we shipped internationally,
even though the range hadn't officially launched yet, as we
were still smoothing out some wrinkles on the website. I gave
Fifi a high-five, which turned into a game of Pat-a-Cake. I was
so proud of her (well, proud of us) for seeing a business
opportunity and seizing it.

'Grab your clutch bag, Fifi my darling,' I told her. 'We're
going for a well-earned pampering session!' I had already
organised for a hotel porter to pack up our wardrobe and
courier my suitcases and boxes back to my house that evening;
I might as well make the most of having someone at my beck
and call. As it was only mid-afternoon, I had a few hours to
kill and knew the perfect place to do it – Venustus Beauty and
Body Lab, my favourite spa in Paddington.

On the drive there I called ahead to book an appointment:
a hot rock massage for me and then a St Tropez spray tan.
The latter was all-important. I am usually regimental with
my Sunday spray tans and weekly blow-dries, but that had all
gone out the window as I regressed into a Glastonbury grub.
I usually travel everywhere with ModelCo 'Tan in a Can'.
A quick spritz and you look like you've just returned from

Barbados, even if you haven't left your desk in twelve months. But it had mysteriously gone missing from my handbag during the Savannah photo shoot (I'm not pointing the finger!). After a week of British weather, despite a few days of welcome sunshine, I looked like an extra from Twilight. There is nothing worse, in my opinion, than seeing your natural skin colour. Call me superficial, but I feel happier, more confident and even more energetic when my skin is closer to mahogany than neutral. It's not vanity, it's evolution. Who wants to be a plain Jane when they can be a blonde juggernaut?

You know how you associate certain smells with your childhood? For me it was my mother baking fresh bread and my father smoking cigars out his bedroom window. Well, I'm sure that when Fifi is older the smell of spray tan will give her a warm fuzzy feeling, reminding her of me and the precious moments we shared.

It's no secret this Queen Bee likes to be bronzed, but Fifi is also a tanning booth veteran. From the first time she watched me having a spray tan, standing like a starfish in a paper g-string, she's been utterly transfixed by the process. Well, wouldn't you be if you were a toddler? I still think it's magical that I can change colour like a chameleon.

My favourite beautician, a curvaceous Italian called Mona, knows the drill by now and is very accommodating. When Fifi and I arrived at Venustus, she led us through to the changing room, handed us both a fluffy robe and also two plastic shower caps. Like a pro, Fifi unwrapped the cap and pulled it over her head, making sure that all her red ringlets were safely tucked away.

My two-year-old then led the way to the tanning booth and took up her position. She even knows the pose to get the best all-over tan: wide legs, arms out to the side, face scrunched up so it wouldn't get in her eyes. As Mona aimed the spray gun at her, Fifi rotated on the spot so that her front and back were covered. Before you report me for child abuse, what my little girl doesn't realise that is it's only air coming out of the spray gun. We only turn on the tanner when it's my go. What, did you really think I'm that bad a mother? I don't plan to let Fifi have a real fake tan until she's at least twelve years old . . . or maybe ten. I'm not like one of those stage mums from *Toddlers and Tiaras*.

As I was pummelled with hot stones, Fifi also had a massage. Although she's far too ticklish for a full body, so she prefers to opt for a foot rub and pedicure. As I watched my daughter wriggling with happiness at the hands of the beauty therapist, I made a decision – I was no longer going to feel guilty or apologise for the lifestyle I had made for my daughter. So most two-year-olds don't spend their days at business meetings and spa treatments, but does that mean it's wrong? In a couple of years, Fifi would be at school and we wouldn't be able to share these magical moments. I didn't want to look back and regret holding out on her.

Okay, my daughter prefers mud masks to mud pies and conference calls to crayoning, but every kid is different. Her social media profile happened by accident and was never meant to be a commercial venture. I would shut down her Instagram account in an instant if it harmed her health or her happiness, but you can see from her smile that she's in her element.

As we left Venustus after three hours of pampering, we both had a skip in our step and our cheeks were glowing (not just from the fake tan).

'Guess what? We're going to see Daddy,' I told Fifi, who wiggled excitedly in her car seat.

Now, I was ready to face the world again. Now I was ready to face my husband.

19

Some boyfriends break up with girls via text message, others hide behind emails. I'll never forget when Anya's last boyfriend broke up with her with a meme of Hermione Granger with the flashing caption: 'Want to see me do a magic trick? POOF! You're single.' We didn't know whether to hate him or admire his creativity.

It was now exactly five weeks since Michael had been offered the job, which meant it was time to tell his prospective boss – and his wife – the decision. Was I about to become a 'living-away partner' or a 'long-distance co-parent'? Forget digital correspondence and virtual animation, my husband gave me his answer using the medium of home decoration.

Even though I'd told Michael that Fifi and I would be home – for good – around dinnertime that night, I didn't expect him to be there to greet us. My husband had warned me that he'd be stuck late at the office. Something to do with a bear in the market. I swear he just tosses around this jargon when he wants to confuse me.

So I wasn't surprised when I pulled into our driveway and saw that Michael's Mercedes was missing. I was, however, surprised by a new addition to our front porch. What the . . . ? Above the doorway hung a huge American flag, the stars and stripes blowing in the wind as if they were taunting me. That would be a yes then . . . he was definitely going.

I very nearly turned around and drove straight back out of there. I could deal with this situation in the same way I'd dealt with Savannah Jagger finding a second agent – pre-empt the dump by pretending to dump him first. It could work! I could pretend that I'd never even been back to the house and just text Michael a 'Sorry, it's not working out' message. At least then I'd look like I was in control of the situation (although just thinking about it made my heart feel like it was being trampled by a mob of shoe addicts at a Louboutin sample sale).

The problem was I had nowhere to go. I didn't even have Shelley's apartment to flee to, as my BFF was still in London with her Glastonbury souvenir. She'd also stopped leaving a spare key under her doormat since her neighbour – a very judgemental and disgruntled vegan – had broken into her apartment and squirted her fox-fur coat with ketchup. I really, really didn't want to go back to living in a hotel – the novelty had totally worn off.

I had no other option. It was time to face my new reality and move back into my matrimonial home . . . even if that was as a single mother. On the way through the front door, I ripped down the American flag and tossed it to the ground, resisting the urge to stomp on it. Immediately, Fifi picked it up, threw it over her head and ran around 'whoooing' like a ghost. It was fitting fancy dress, seeing as my relationship was dead and buried.

The house was, as Jackson had promised, an absolute masterpiece. If I hadn't been suffering from the early symptoms of heartbreak, I'd have been skipping between each room right now screaming, 'I DIE, I DIE.'

It was an oasis of cooling, calming monochrome balanced with bold and quirky statement pieces. That neon-green Perspex sculpture of a lizard would be way over the top if it wasn't set against a solid grey backdrop. It was kind of like a metaphor for my relationship with Michael. I was the attention-seeking statement-maker, and he was the reliable, solid, stable neutral. That balance was why our relationship worked. Why hadn't I appreciated that until it was too late?

As I walked around the house, leaving Fifi to get reacquainted with her toy collection, I tried not to become nostalgic for the happy memories. The kitchen, where Michael had helped me write The Talent Hive's business plan. The bathroom, where he'd held my hair back during my morning sickness. The bedroom, where . . . well, we don't need to go into those details.

And then there was Michael's study. I noticed he'd left the door slightly open, which was unusual as he normally locked it for security reasons. But hang on a second, why could I see baby-blue wallpaper? I had specifically told Jackson to decorate the study in yellow, because I'd read an article in *BRW* magazine that claimed it increased productivity and concentration.

I hesitantly pushed open the door. OMG! There'd clearly been a huge mistake. Michael's desk had been replaced with a brand-new oak baby's crib, his filing cabinets had been swapped for a nappy-changing table, and the bookshelves where he usually filed his stock market reports in chronological order had been removed. Instead, the far wall was covered in a modern-art montage of Disney characters (I recognised graffiti artist Sid Tapia's handiwork). All in all, it was a nursery fit for little Prince George . . . except we didn't have a baby in our household.

As I tried to marshal my thoughts, I heard a cough behind me. I spun on my heel. 'Michael! What the hell are you doing here? I'm so sorry about this room,' I blathered. 'I'm going to call Jackson right now and get it fixed. I don't know how he could have got my instructions so wrong, but I'll put it right . . .'

Halfway through my rambling apology, I remembered something. 'Actually, it doesn't matter, does it?' I said cattily. 'I saw the flag. Well, I was hardly going to miss it. I may as well leave the freaking study as it is . . . or I could turn it into a spare room, or a home gym or something. Maybe I could give Fifi her own study for her business empire. It's not like you're going to be needing it . . .'

Michael was looking at me with an odd expression. I couldn't work out if he was amused or nervous. 'Jasmine Lewis, will you please be quiet for one moment?' he interrupted me, although his voice wasn't unkind and he took my hand in his. 'I was the one who told Jackson to do this,' he continued. 'I had an emergency meeting with him last week and he kindly agreed to make some last-minute changes. Jazzy Lou, I'm so, so sorry. I never should have even considered the job without consulting you first. You're my world, you and Fifi, and you'll always be my priority. You're also not the only person who can chuck around ultimatums. Yesterday I told Chad Turner that I'd only take the job if I could do it remotely from Sydney. It's a very hip way to work apparently, very Gen Y, very Google, and he actually loved the idea. I'll still have to go to America for five days out of the month, but that just means you'll get a constant supply of J.Crew and Hershey bars . . .'

It was the perfect reconciliation speech – an apology mixed with a compliment and a touch of bribery. My husband should go into PR himself. I always say a pitch should be as good as a selfie – clear, well lit, and reflecting the most flattering angle.

But what was with the freaking study? I gestured to our surroundings. 'Michael, why have you built a nursery?' My sentence was punctuated by the toot of a toy train, which was whirring around a track fixed to the wall above our heads. There'd been a similar train at Glastonbury delivering tequila shots. Groan! I was having a flashback!

Michael stood in the centre of the room like an artist presenting his materpiece. 'Well, I know you're a fan of big, bold publicity stunts,' he said, 'so I thought I might be more likely to convince you if I put in some extra effort. Jazzy Lou, I suspect you believe that I think you're a terrible mother. But that couldn't be further from the truth. While you were in England I did some soul-searching. If I'm honest, sometimes I'm a bit jealous of the great job you do with Fifi. I could never compete, but that's just something I need to come to terms with.'

He picked up a toy Action Man from the nappy-changing table and pulled the trigger of his gun. 'Jasmine, you're an amazing mother and the head of our amazing family . . . a family that I'd like to grow bigger. I was thinking . . . I was hoping . . . that we could try for another baby.'

One thing you should know about me – and publicists in general – is that when we set our minds to something we always deliver, whether that's media coverage, a celebrity ambassador . . . or a baby.

As I lay on the sonographer's table, Michael and I held our breath and waited for the doctor to distinguish limbs from genitals. I stared at the grey blob on the screen, thinking it looked more like an alien than a baby, and then the doctor uttered a sentence that made Michael's eyes water: 'Congratulations, you're having a boy.'

We let Fifi break the news on our behalf by posting the sonogram shot to her Instagram page:

> This is my baby brother. I am going to call him #Henry. Heck, I'm going to be busy managing Instagram for not just one but two Queen Bee offspring come April.

I'd made the mistake of telling her she could pick the name for her new brother. I was thinking Ralph (Lauren), Oscar (de la Renta) or Alexander (Wang), but no, she clearly wanted her brother to be more down to earth than that. Sadly, her favourite show is *Horrible Henry*. Oh well, I had six months to talk her out of it before he made an appearance.

That social media announcement was the first of Fifi's Instagram posts that didn't get a single negative comment. Perhaps our critics were coming around to the idea of a two-year-old Insta-star. Or maybe nobody is cruel enough to troll an unborn foetus. Either way, it was a milestone and one I chose to see as positive.

It was also the first Instagram post for as long as I could remember that Hayden Smith didn't 'like' or comment on. Flirting with a married woman is one thing, but flirting with a mother-to-be would be a new moral low.

Then I noticed a comment under the photograph from a familiar face – Tessa Blow. She'd changed her profile photo, dyed her hair blonder and looked even more of a Vegas Showgirl than ever (sorry to be catty, I blame my hormones). For the past ten weeks since I'd come back from Glastonbury, my father had been pestering me with 'We need to talk' text messages that I'd been ignoring. He was texting me four or five times a day now. What could possibly be so freaking important?

When I read Tessa's comment, the answer revealed itself. As my hands shook with astonishment, my Chanel charm bracelet jingled like an alarm bell. Was my future stepmother (eugh!) really saying what I thought she was saying?

Amazing news, Jazzy Lou! Your dad and I are over the moon. And what perfect timing! Our babies will be in the same class at school. Two new additions to the family. See you at prenatal yoga, darling!

OH MY GOD!!!

ALSO FROM ALLEN & UNWIN

STRICTLY CONFIDENTIAL

ROXY JACENKO

Meet Jasmine Lewis, the smart young publicist trying to work her way up from the bottom in Sydney's hottest PR company. She's done the coffee runs, the dry-cleaning pickups, the 5 a.m. starts, the 11 p.m. finishes. But still her evil boss Diane Wilderstein is never happy. So when Jasmine finds herself being summoned to Diane's office early one morning, she knows something's got to give. Luckily for Jasmine, fate lends a hand and helps her escape from the evil Diane to launch a fabulous new career.

That should be a dream come true, right? Or is it the start of a whole new world of nightmares?

'Ever wondered what really goes on behind the slick facade of the PR world? Strictly Confidential will knock your Manolos off!' Gemma Crisp, former editor of CLEO

ISBN 978 1 74237 757 5

THE RUMOUR MILL

ROXY JACENKO

Jazzy Lou is back and busier than ever!

Queen Bee, her fabulous PR firm, is going from strength to strength with an ever-expanding roster of clients, including the hottest new International Designer.

At home, Jazzy has her hands full with her baby girl Fifi, as well as the planning of her upcoming wedding to Michael. But just as everything seems to be falling into place, Jazzy discovers that her old boss, the evil Diane Wilderstein, has resurfaced and has her heart set on poaching Jazzy's Queen Bee clients. Meanwhile, someone is trying to bring her down by circulating a poisonous voicemail to ALL of Sydney's media!

Will they succeed in destroying everything Jazzy has worked so hard for? Or will Jazzy find a way to save herself and Queen Bee? Sit back and enjoy this fast-paced peek inside the glamorous world of Sydney's hottest PR agency.

'All the gossip you'd expect from Sydney's PR Queen.'
Bronwyn McCahon, editor of *Cosmopolitan*

ISBN 978 1 76011 137 3